FORESHADOW

Trapped in her own mind

LEENA ALTHEKAIR

© **Leena Nasser Althekair, 2018**
  King Fahd National Library Cataloging-in-Publication Data

Althekair, Leena Nasser
  Foreshadow: Trapped in her own mind. / Leena Nasser
Althekair – Jeddah , 2018

    ..p ; ..cm
    ISBN: 978-603-02-6449-0

    1-Short Story   I-Title
    813.019531 dc   1439/4578

        L.D. no. 1439/4578
        ISBN: 978-603-02-6449-0

DEDICATION

To mom and dad. I owe everything I am today to you after
God. Nothing I can ever do can repay the countless
sacrifices you've given up for me. I love you.

CONTENTS

1 CLUELESS

I zipped up the side of my dress and shuffled to the mirror. It didn't look the way I imagined, but it was still nice. It was *crucial* I make a good impression. Why? Because it was my mom's second cousin's wedding, which meant I was going to meet my mom's relatives I don't see a lot, which meant I had to be the perfect girl they had always heard about.

Mom says I'm overreacting and that they'll like me the way I am because they're family. You see, that's my problem: I tend to overthink stuff.

I inhaled deeply and looked again. There I was, in my lilac, knee-length dress, beige wedges and clutch bag, gold accessories and brown, curled hair. Mom would've said I was gorgeous. Elora would've said I was "queen." Michael would've said I was irresistible. But all I saw was an out-of-place bow, uneven eyeliner wings, puffy hair, and stained heels. Was it even there? I didn't know anymore.

Mom's reflection in the mirror made me turn around and meet her smile. "You look gorgeous," she assured me.

I looked back to the mirror, but I couldn't see what she meant. "Are you sure? I think it's kinda tight from here, and the bow's uneven from this side. The shoes don't match that much either—"

"Calm down." She wrapped her arms around me. "You look fine. Stop worrying so much."

Trust me, I wish I could.

"Now come on, Dad and Maha are in the car waiting. You know how your father will get angry if we're late."

I sighed. "Do I *have* to go?" I really didn't like Mom's distant relatives that much, and frankly, I was kinda nervous.

She gave me a warm hug and then looked straight into my eyes. "You'll do fine. Just socialize and get to know them better. Listen to their conversations and try to join in." And with that, she led me down the stairs and out the front door. "You'll do great," she whispered as she opened the front passenger door and got in. I got into the backseat wearing the widest fake-realistic smile I could manage.

She twisted in her seat to have a better view of me. "You'll do wonderful." She smiled as Dad pulled out of the driveway and onto the street.

"Ready to dazzle your cousins, Meg?" Dad winked. I

smiled brightly and nodded, even though I felt a bit queasy. All the same, I looked at the full half of the cup; maybe I'd meet someone my age, or play cool new wedding games since it was trending these days, or find exotic new entrées I could try. I was determined to make the best of it, even if my stomach disagreed.

***

To me, the most magical moment in a wedding is when the bride walks in. I literally feel as if it's real magic, with her white dress and translucent veil. It's as if there's actual glitter surrounding her, illuminating her face in a golden hue. The way everybody looks at her, and how her smile gives away how shy but happy she is. It's the scene I await whenever I set foot in a wedding venue. The truly magical moment for every bride and spectator. Yep, I do believe it's real, actual magic. And this one was no different.

Shortly after the ceremony, people were dancing and laughing, dotting every inch of the ballroom, congratulating the newlyweds and their family. Surprisingly, I was congratulated too! I mean, sure, I'm family, but I never would've seen that coming.

"Meghan, dearie, there you are!" I swiveled and saw my favorite of mom's aunts.

"Aunt Lindsey!" I smiled and hugged her tightly. I felt a teensy bit better that I met one relative I didn't dislike.

"You look fabulous, sweetie!" She smiled as we pulled

away from our hug. "My, my, I do say . . . where'd you get this?" She gestured for me to twirl as she took a step back. "Meghan, that looks marvelous on you! You totally make it work"—cue blush—"and that makeup is on point! You did it yourself?"

"Yeah, but it's nothing professional." I blushed an even brighter shade of scarlet. Getting a compliment from your great-aunt, who was also a best-selling fashion designer, was awesome. "Thanks!"

"How do you like the décor?" she asked as she targeted her attention to the shawls draped on the seats and the rose pillars placed around the grand hall.

"It's *perfect*." I hesitated. "It was you who decorated it, wasn't it?"

Aunt Lindsey's lips formed a huge grin. "I knew you'd recognize my style! Anyway, I've got to go. Being the groom's aunt means business!"

My tiny bubble of hope popped as she walked away to greet more guests. I might have been wishing that she just hung out with me.

Other than that, I felt pretty much bored.

Maha was playing with a few other kids her age. Phew; another responsibility off my shoulders. Mom was laughing and being the social butterfly she is. Everybody loves her. She strikes up the funniest conversations and *everyone* wants to befriend her.

I wish I was half as good.

I settled with taking a seat at the farthest edge of the ballroom. That didn't do me any good either.

I kept feeling people's stares penetrating me and silently judging me; my appearance, the way I sat, everything. What would Mom tell me? Probably to go talk to people. But my main goal was to avoid contact with all humans for now.

"Meghan, *get out there* and talk!" Mom suddenly appeared by my side and urged me. See? "If I see you on your phone one more time, you'll be sorry."

"But I don't want to talk to people," I whined. "I don't even like them!"

"You never talked to them!"

"Yeah, and I'd like to keep it that way."

"*Meghan . . .*"

"Fine . . . I'll *try* to socialize."

"Stop playing the role of the grumpy anti-social teen. You're barely fourteen."

"I'm not playing the role, it's my personality."

She gave me a look that told me I had crossed the line.

"Okay," I sighed in defeat. "I'll talk with Aunt Nora's daughters."

"Wonderful." She gave a slight, almost invisible smile

and went up to some other group of ladies.

Honestly, I would've preferred being at home and binge-watching *Full House* in my pajamas with Candy. So much for a lazy Sunday.

Hiding my phone under the table, I tried refreshing and re-refreshing my social media account, but for some reason, *nobody* was online.

I was lost in my thoughts when a tall girl wearing a silver dress sat down next to me.

"You're Meghan, correct?" she smiled. Great, another person who knew me and I had no idea who they were! Come to think of it, that was the case with nearly everyone I'd met today . . .

"Yep, that's me!" I could smell the dreaded question coming along.

"Well, Meg, do you know who I am?"

There it was.

I shook my head, not feeling the slightest bit of guilt. I barely knew anyone.

The laugh that followed indicated she wasn't disappointed that I had zero clue about her.

"Well of course, I thought you wouldn't. You've only seen me once before. I'm Riley, sister of the groom."

Well, she seemed nice. I didn't think I'd mind talking to

her.

"Nice to meet you," I replied. *Seriously*? She literally came up to me to have a friendly conversation and the best I could think of was *nice to meet you*?

"Have you had fun tonight?"

"Yeah, I did enjoy listening to Aunt Nora's tales." Which, frankly, wasn't a lie. I wasn't *eavesdropping*, just listening to the conversation from afar. "And the ballroom looks amazing."

"Yeah, Aunt Lindsey did a fabulous job."

Was she going to leave now? Did she come because she felt bad for me? Was she silently judging me and my stupid replies?

"What grade are you in?"

My favorite question.

"Oh, I begin high school next August."

"Nice! I'm a senior in college."

College? Really? She seemed too nice to be a twenty-something grump. At least that's what Michael is, and he's barely a college freshman.

"How do you feel about school? I don't mean to burst your bubble, but IRL high school is nothing like *High School Musical*."

I had to laugh. That was *my* kind of sense of humor.

"Yeah, I figured. It's exciting, but pretty stressful."

"You'll do fine," she assured me. "All you have to do is pay close attention to your time management and be ready day by day. Procrastination is your worst enemy."

"Feels like my best friend nowadays," I sighed. She laughed.

"Please, it's everybody's nowadays. What else have we got to do during summer?"

"Social media exists for a reason."

"True," she smiled, and shook her head. "Media, ugh."

Who knew I could find a friend out of my dreaded cousins?

For a person who doesn't particularly like talking to people, this was not as bad as I thought. The small talk went on to become a full-length conversation as we talked about everything from Elvis Presley to our favorite cheesecake flavor. Sure, there was about an 8-year age difference, but I felt like I had known her for *ages*.

2 FRESH BEGINNINGS

A heavy sigh escaped my lips as I stood in front of my open closet. I had *nothing* to wear. I put together an outfit in my mind last night, but it didn't turn out the way I imagined it would. GREAT.

It was the first day of school already. It was like the two months since the wedding flew by and *BAM!* Back-to-school commercials are *everywhere*. They make me sick. I don't mind going to school but for God's sake, please stop rubbing it in my face.

As I tried on the sixth outfit, my phone's screen lit up. A message? At 6:00 a.m.? That isn't from Elora?

RILEY: Good luck! Go show 'em who's boss this year! :)

That was oddly nice of her. I confided a lot in her about how nervous I was. As usual, I kept worrying more and more as the beginning of the school year neared. She gave me tons of advice, and even told me a few of her mischievous stories. It did help me, and I was touched she took the time to encourage me.

MEGHAN: Thanks! I plan to :)

I quickly replied and settled with my outfit; a cantaloupe-orange tank top with a white crocheted sweater and faded navy jeans. Riley told me to dress like "me," and this was the "me-est" thing. It seemed a little comforting knowing I had an older opinion.

I grabbed my matching crocheted handbag and dashed downstairs to where Mom was making breakfast.

"Morning, sweetheart," she called from below the counter. "Had a good night's sleep?"

"Refreshing," I smiled as I made my way towards her.

"Um, you plan to go to school, on your first day, looking like *that*?" she asked as she reappeared from under the counter. The uncertain look on her face made me question my outfit once more.

"Why? Is the sweater too much? Should I switch the tank top?" The endless list of fashion don'ts I have committed ran through my head.

She gave me a small smile and gestured at the entrance mirror. "See for yourself."

I did as I was told and—*aw, man.* I did it again. I laughed as I tossed my bag onto the couch and made my way upstirs.

"You don't think I'd let you go to school with morning hair, did you?"

I always got dressed then did my hair. Most days, I forgot the latter. I headed upstairs for a "First Day of School" hair-and-makeup routine.

***

MEGHAN: We're in the car. Don't be late or mom will change her mind. HURRY UP!!!

I hurriedly texted Elora as Mom grabbed her keys and shooed Maha and Michael outside. Yes, all our names begin with the letter *M*, I know. Cute though, right?

I slipped my phone into my handbag before Mom told me off for using technology early in the morning. The usual morning hubbub of the Bakers included Michael running back in to fetch his binder, Maha panicking about some problem or the other, and me, standing by the door all ready with my schoolbag. Except I didn't have a schoolbag today.

First day, no books!

After twenty minutes or so we finally managed to get outside, where I found Elora leaning on the car hood, her auburn hair flowing in the wind. I had a feeling she intended to look that way.

"I thought you said you were in the car," she smirked as Mom unlocked the car. "Tsk, tsk, I've been standing here for half an hour!"

"Please, I sent you that text barely fifteen minutes ago. Besides, you and I both know how long you take to get ready."

"I have no idea what you're talking about," she said with a hair flip, and climbed into Dad's Explorer, me right behind.

As soon as we all climbed in, Mom began her pep talk.

"All of you are starting a new year and a new stage in your life." She turned to look at Elora, Maha, and me as well. "And I'm sure you'll get this year off to a great start."

"And Maha will dominate middle school!" Maha pumped her fist in the air.

"*All of you* will dominate," Mom laughed. "Just remember; be confident. Everything new is an adventure. Who feels confident?"

"MEEE!" we all yelled in unison, even Michael.

"Perfect." Mom turned back to the front. "Mike, watch

12

out for that pothole!"

"Mom, I have a driver's license. I think I know how to drive."

"Just looking out for you," she said in her baby-Mom voice and pinched his cheek as he ducked out of the way.

"*Mom*! Okay, who's ready to sing along with me?"

As Maha, Michael, and Mom blasted into the beginning of a song, Elora turned to me wearing a frown.

"What?" I raised an eyebrow.

"You picked your outfit."

"And?"

"You didn't ask for my advice."

"So?"

"*So*?" She seemed agitated. "You always ask for my fashion advice! Why didn't you snap me like you usually do?" But then her expression changed. "Did I do anything?"

"What? No!" I was baffled. "Why would you think such a thing?"

"I dunno." She crossed her arms and slumped lower in her seat. "I thought you were mad at me or something, since you didn't ask me like you usually do."

Okay, now I get it. I used to (and still do) ask Elora how my outfit is before every outing. I guess she felt I was

13

upset or something since I kinda ditched that habit this morning, which usually meant I was upset.

"Lora, seriously, you're my *best friend*," I reassured her. "If I was mad at you, I would've said it to your face. I wouldn't have been silent about it. In fact, I would've made you feel bad until you apologized."

She couldn't help but laugh.

"I'm serious! Besides, a silly snapstreak doesn't define our friendship, am I right?"

"I guess so." She sat up. "Actually, I'm proud you made a fashion choice without me! Thank God you stopped worrying about how you look."

"Hold your horses; it took me forty-five minutes to put this together!"

"Better than the hour you took last week."

"Point made."

***

It took no time to finally reach Celestial High (and its twin middle school), and just as fast we had clambered out of the car and onto the sidewalk.

"I can't believe I get to go to school with MEGHAN! FINALLY!" Maha squealed as I waved goodbye to Mom.

I laughed and pulled her into a hug. "I'm pumped too. Now go show Celestial Middle what it's been missing!"

"Way ahead of ya." She waved goodbye and ran up to a group of girls huddled by the middle school entrance.

"Feels weird not to go there like we usually do, huh?" Elora commented.

"Yeah," I half-replied, half-stared at the star-studded archway where middle schoolers laughed and lounged on the ivory benches dotting the front of the middle school campus.

"Come on, we're this way."

I followed Elora to where it was known among middle schoolers as the "High and Mighty League," or HML.

Wow, finally a high schooler, I thought. *Who knew I was gonna make it this far?*

The entrance archway was way bigger. It sported a galactic palette with white "star" specks all over. Beyond were navy blue and purple benches, dotted across the campus. Even the sidewalks were a baby-yellow pavement, reflecting the hazy morning sun.

"The high school VP sure knows her designing," Elora commented as we both took in the amazing view.

"Well then, let's do this." I linked my arm through hers and together we walked through the archway. We were officially high schoolers. Which was why I couldn't help squealing.

"Keep it down! Don't make a bad first impression!"

Elora hissed half-jokingly.

A friendly looking blonde girl walked up to us. She was wearing a normal crop top and high-waisted black pants, but the clipboard in her hand gave her a sort of important look. She wore a beret, too, and frankly, that's all the evidence I needed to realize she was student body president.

"Hello there, you two! I recognize you from last year's collaborated play!" She tapped her pen against her chin for a while. "Anne and Teresa, right?"

"Those were our stage names," Elora laughed. "I'm Elora, she's Meghan."

"Nice to meet you! I'm Elizabeth; just call me Liz. Welcome to the high school section of Celestial School, or should I say, HML."

"You know about that?" I laughed.

"I was a middle schooler once, you know." She winked. "Anyway, I have the class list here to guide you and"—she traced her finger down the clipboard—"you guys are in nine-2. First class down the right loop. See you later!" And with that, she marched off to meet other newcomers.

"She seems nice," I commented as we made our way to the right entrance. Celestial Middle was built to resemble an infinity shape; classes lined on the outer edges, cafeteria in one circle, staff rooms/admin offices in the other. The high school section wasn't any different, except the décor was way more awesome.

16

"She *is* nice," Elora replied. "Liz has won 'most likely to befriend everyone' three times in a row! And she is friends with every high schooler at Celestial High. It's a shame it's her senior year."

Elora knew everything about everyone in middle school, and apparently, she intended to keep up that habit. It came in useful at times, others just downright ridiculous.

We went in through the right door and into the right loop, where ninth- and tenth-grade students filled the celestial-colored hallways.

"LORA! MEG! OVER HERE!"

I knew that voice all too well. Alex was waving at us from the doorway of nine-2, motioning for us to come in.

"How lucky are we that we ended up all together?" she said with a smile.

Sure enough, almost all last year's eight-2s were present; only two unfamiliar faces. I waved from the hallway and the class erupted in cheers.

"Queen Anne and Duchess Teresa, *do* come in!" She bowed as we mock strode into class, our noses in the air.

"Seriously, last year's play was a *huge* success," Penny agreed. "And you two slayed these roles!"

"I know," Elora replied with a hair flip.

"Hey, guys." Talia emerged from the back of the class, an unfamiliar girl in each hand. "We've got newcomers!"

17

"Well then, WELCOME TO NINE-2!" we all cheered, and gave them jazz hands.

"I'm Meghan Baker, and you are?" I smiled as I extended my hand.

"Olivia Thomas," one of them smiled and took my hand, shaking it pleasantly.

"Sarah May," the other one replied as she, too, shook my hand, but in a more timid way.

"I'm Elora Black! Welcome to nine-2. Trust me, you're in the best class," Elora said with a wink.

"I'm Penelope." Penny jumped in front of the new girls and smiled. "But everyone calls me Penny. Nice to meet ya!"

Soon enough, everybody was introducing themselves with a warm smile before the deafening school bell marked the beginning of first period. Since there was no assigned seating, I picked the desk most convenient for me before Elora sat next to me with a wink. Natural for us to sit next to each other, right?

The classroom was arranged just like any other class; three columns, six desks in each row, making twelve pairs and twenty-four students total.

A young woman with waist-length brown hair walked in. She wore an elbow-length *Slytherin* shirt with mint green stilettos. She had blonde highlights and wore a black headband to complement her black jeans.

I was confused, because why would a senior walk in when our homeroom teacher was supposed to be here any minute?

She set her purse on the teacher's desk as the entire class fell silent. Pin-drop silence, to be exact. She wrote something on the whiteboard and turned to face us, her smile complementing her fabulous, yet simple makeup.

"Good morning, nine-2. I'm Avery Benson, and I will be your English teacher, in addition to being your homeroom teacher," she announced as she leaned against the teacher's desk.

"*You're* our homeroom teacher?" Elora accidentally blurted out.

"Yes, I thought that's what I just said," she said with a small laugh.

Whispers broke out among the students. *Who is she? Why is she dressed like that? Is she serious or is it a lame senior prank?*

Avery (still not sure if she was a Ms. or Mrs.) laughed at our expressions and shook her head in disbelief.

"Yes, it does seem weird that I'm a teacher, but trust me, I am a certified one too. This is actually my first official job."

"Um, I hope you don't mind me asking, Teacher, but are you married?" Penny asked, her face blushing at her own question.

"Goodness, no! If I was, my husband wouldn't have let me leave the house like this."

"How old are you?" Elora prompted, apparently insistent on finding out as much as she could.

"Twenty-four."

Twenty-four? That's the youngest a teacher's ever been! That is, if you don't count lousy high schoolers substituting at times.

"Wait, so you're a *Potterhead?"* Olivia Thomas asked, apparently still awed by who this teacher was.

"Doesn't the shirt convey the message?" she asked as she gestured at the snake on her abdomen.

"Oh my gosh, you're a Slytherin too?" Jessica couldn't help blurting out.

"Too? Who else is a Slytherin here?"

Elora's hand shot up just as fast as she had asked the question, along with a few other girls.

"Nice! Well, like all Slytherins, there's something you should know about me," she began as she paced around the front of the class. "I'm as sweet as pie, and don't mind a few, *minor* misbehaviors in class. But you don't want to get on *my* bad side…"

3 SCIENTIFIC RESEARCH

Day one of high school was an official success. Ms. Avery was even cooler than that. And as any good-natured teacher would do, we chatted away for the first two periods and she even allowed us to snap—*during class.*

The rest of the day went just as great. All the teachers were just as friendly, but not very phone-approving. We spent most of our time babbling away about almost everything.

Mrs. Kartley was an exception, though. Like any high school ever, there had to be that "foe" teacher. She smiled and introduced herself, allowed us to introduce ourselves, and passed out *worksheets.* Her only comment to our objections was that we were in high school, and "just because it's the first day doesn't mean you have an excuse to abandon your education." With that, we spent the next thirty-five minutes filling out papers on climates, landscapes,

21

and ocean currents.

***

"Hey, Lora," I started as we rounded the corner to our block, Maha skipping ahead of us. "Why do you think Mrs. Kartley is so miserable?"

"She probably has a sad past, which unintentionally affects her present personality and influences her decisions," she began in her philosophical tone. "But I know for a fact that she's in her mid-fifties and has sixteen cats at home. Crazy old cat lady, check."

I laughed as we came to a halt in front of her house.

"Are you *sure* you can't spend the day at my place? I literally live across the street," I said as she walked up the pebble walkway.

"Mom has her friends over, and guess who's a butler for the day?" she said with a wave of her hand and a bow.

"Aw, you pitiful thing," I sarcastically replied. "In that case, see you tomorrow."

I waved to her as I crossed the street, Maha in hand. As I turned the key, a loud crash made me rush indoors and check if everything was still in one piece.

"Mom, what's going on?" I yelled with a little fear in my voice.

"Oh, nothing, I'm fine," she called from upstairs. "Just the shampoo bottles." Typical. I couldn't help laughing a bit as I kicked off my shoes and sank into the couch.

As soon as Dad came home we had a family dinner, where Michael had to explain in detail how his first day of college went, then me with my first high school experience, then Maha with her first day of middle school.

Michael was acting eerily suspicious throughout the meal, and as soon he finished his tale, he dashed upstairs. His food even remained untouched. I waited to excuse myself until Dad went upstairs, and tiptoed to where Michael fled off to.

I creaked open the door to his room, but he wasn't there. I was sure I saw him come upstairs, but if he wasn't here then—*the attic.*

One thing I love about Michael is his extreme dedication to science. He's been a physics enthusiast ever since his sophomore year, and after that Sci-Fi convention Dad made us go to two years ago, he'd been set on cracking time travel. Dad convinced Mom to give him the attic as a scientific lab, where he can conduct his experiments all he wants. Frankly speaking, it was wicked.

Remember Dexter's laboratory? It's *nothing* compared to what my big brother made. The entire wooden space was transformed into every time traveler's dream; theories and plans were hung up on every inch of wall available. Every tool he'd ever need was exactly where it should be. Even his and our old science textbooks—along with scientific journals Dad bought him—were neatly stacked on a bookshelf. You'd think you walked into Dr. Frankenstein's lab if you ever visited. Which was why I loved this place so much.

"Hey, big bro." I gently pushed open the trapdoor leading to his lab. "Why were you in such a hurry?"

"Was it obvious?" he called from under a piece of cloth (probably old bedsheets) concealing him—and his invention—from my eyes.

"Uh, you barely touched your food, fast-forwarded through your first day of college, and dashed upstairs as soon as Mom and Dad turned their attention to me."

"Yeah, I guess I was too hasty," he admitted as he emerged from behind the bedsheet. "But it's for a very good reason."

"Explain yourself," I laughed as he, his out-of-control hair, and stained lab coat took a seat in front of his work desk.

"I, my dear Meghan, am this close to cracking the secret of time travel!" he announced as he gathered a few folders and walked up to where I was standing. "It's pretty complicated, but today I joined the after-hours time travel club. We put our heads together and I didn't tell them, but I think I found out how we can go back or forward in time."

"Excuse you, *we?*"

"Yes, we! Aren't we lab partners?"

Okay, so it's true, I may have helped him a few . . . dozen times, but I wasn't prepared for something like this.

"Please, proceed," I replied, suspicion and eagerness visible on my face.

"I won't go into details, because a mere middle-schooler—"

"*High*-schooler."

"—wouldn't understand the complicated methods I've used to reach where I am now," he announced, and thrust the folders into my arms.

"So long story short, I present to you, the *Time Explorer 3000.*" He dramatically pulled off the bedsheet and revealed a human-sized, thin donut with wires and bolts sticking out from every direction, and a seat situated in the middle, where supposedly the "test subject" would be sitting—most probably me.

"You did this *yourself?*" I marveled as I set the folders back down on his desk and carefully found my way across the room through tools and copper strewn on the floor.

"No, I ordered it from Amazon." He rolled his eyes. "What do you think? I've been working on this beauty for over a year now. Ever wonder why I didn't attend the wedding with you guys?"

"You left your family for a chunk of *metal?* Tsk, tsk, I thought you were better than this, Michael *Timothy* Baker."

"Oh, zip it," he replied with a playful shove as he went behind the machine.

"When will it be ready for use?" I asked as I took a seat inside the metallic donut. It felt comfortable, despite its iron-y appearance.

"As soon as I apply what I've collected today, it'll be ready for a test-drive. In about, say, a week or two."

"And let me guess; who'll be the test subject?"

"Candy, of course."

"*Are you mental?*" I almost yelled, standing up. "No way you're laying a finger on my precious cat. I've had her since I was a little girl, and I don't plan on losing her anytime soon."

"Usually scientists use lab rats to conduct experiments on, and Candy's the closest I can get."

"Why don't you buy an actual rat, then?"

"That's not a bad idea." He stopped and rubbed his chin in thought. "I'll just have to convince Dad."

"What about Mom?"

"Dad will take care of that." He winked as he flipped open the folders of earlier and scribbled down a few things.

"Good luck, Dr. Michaelstein," I mocked as I squeezed myself behind his desk. "Whatcha doing, anyway?"

"What? Oh, just a few minor adjustments." Then he looked at me. "You *will* be helping me, right? I know it's the first week of *high school*, but you'll still make time for our experimental afternoons . . ."

"Of course." I gave him a light punch on the arm. "I love spending afternoons with you. I'd even leave homework if I had to."

"No thanks, I don't want Mom and Dad blaming me for your academic setback." He laughed. "But thanks."

"No problem."

***

At sunset, I was helping Dad weed the flowerbeds on our front lawn. I usually did it with Mom every six months, but I guess Dad was buttering her up for a weekend out with his friends or something.

"So, how was school today?" he attempted to start a conversation.

"Dad, you already asked me that." I laughed. "How was work for *you* today?"

"Same old, same old," he sighed. Honestly, I felt bad for him. He was working hard every day of the week—including weekends. I just wished I could help him. "What's up with Michael today?"

"You noticed too?"

"Of course! And I also noticed you went after him just

as I excused myself," he said with a wink.

"He said he joined some after-school science club and got a new idea for his . . . time-traveling machine." I was gonna say "Time Explorer 3000," but I guessed maybe Michael would want to do that himself.

"Really?" He stopped tackling a rather large ground ivy.

Again, I tried to limit it as much as possible, because Michael would've loved to do that himself.

Dad's interested in time travel too, which makes them the perfect scientific duo. If it wasn't for his job, Dad would've spent all his afternoons up in that attic/lab. I've even heard him consider quitting his job and becoming a full-time scientist if Michael succeeds.

I thought about the lab rat we discussed earlier, and thought maybe Michael would owe me one.

"Hey, Dad—when I was up in the attic earlier, Mike and I were discussing his time-traveling machine."

"How is it coming along?"

"He seems almost finished actually." And on that note, I really *did* grasp his attention. "Which is why he needs a test subject."

"I thought you usually volunteered to try out his experiments."

"Yes, but not in situations like *this*. I mean, mind-reading helmets and dream-recording headbands were all right, but this is too risky. What if something goes wrong?"

"Hm, you're right . . . I guess Candy will do it then."

"No!" I blurted out.

He looked startled.

"Uh, I mean, why risk my poor cat? Wouldn't something else work just as well? Like, I don't know, a lab rat?"

"Young lady, are you trying to convince me to buy Mike *lab rats*?" He raised an eyebrow at me. *Busted*. Well, it's better that I come off as honest.

"Yes, actually," I began. "I mean, Mike's really getting into it. He's even picked out his subjects in college already and planned his master's and PhD as well. It only seems fair that we get him proper test subjects."

He sat on the grass cross-legged. "Proceed."

"I also know that he's gonna take good care of them—in *cages*. He'll feed them and keep them in good shape, unless and until an experiment requires otherwise."

He just kept nodding and thoroughly considering it; I could tell from his face. Meghan persuasion mode was on.

"You could buy him just two at first. Then, if and until one dies, we can get another. Besides, how expensive are rats gonna be?"

"Okay, I'm convinced," he nodded. "But, how do we

make sure they're not diseased? We don't want a Black Plague here in our place—and the entire city."

"Exactly," I smiled. "Which is why we'll buy lab *mice* instead of actual rats."

"I like the way you think." He went back to wrestling the ivy. "But how am I going to convince your mom?"

"I think that's up to you to accomplish," I smirked, and skipped inside.

"Where are you going? We're not done yet!" he yelled after me.

"Off to get us snacks!" I yelled back as I dropped my gloves by the door and glided into the kitchen.

"Hey, sis," Michael smiled as he balanced a bag of chips, Hershey's kisses, and a few other snacks on his arms. "I was thinking I'd try to tackle Dad tomorrow, before heading for school."

"No need." I smiled as I took the mini pretzels from him and grabbed two juice boxes from the fridge.

"What? Then how am I supposed to—oh, *you didn't.*"

"I did!" The smile penetrated my face as I walked back out. "You'll be getting your lab *mice* by next weekend."

The look on his face was all the thank you I needed. He was so happy, I could tell that it'd be the perfect example to use when he wouldn't let me borrow something from him . . .

"Pretzels?" I offered Dad as I kneeled beside him.

"Yes, please!" He opened wide as I popped a few into his mouth. "Okay, tho now that you've perthuaded me to get you mithe, I need a favor fwom you," he managed to say as he chewed.

"Let me guess, you wanna have a guys' weekend next week?"

"The week after, but I was—hey, how'd you know?"

I couldn't help laughing. "Well, you are weeding the garden."

"What? No! I'm just doing this to lift a bit of weight off her shoulders. I was gonna use yo—uh . . . *convince* you to help me persuade her."

"Sure, Dad," I laughed as I popped a few more mini pretzels in his mouth and took a gulp from my mango nectar. "Whatever you say."

4 SOUR FACE

Frankly, I enjoy geography immensely. It fascinates me how two places, just a few kilometers apart, can have a massive difference in landforms. How the atmosphere affects climates. Why and how mountains form. When did rivers begin to run through land. I just love it *so much*.

And Mrs. Kartley's making it hard for me. I mean, it's like she has something against me. It's been two weeks of school already and every time I raise my hand to answer, *she ignores me*. Like, she'd look me in the eyes, then go on and say how pitiful she feels that the class knows nothing.

I once tried to talk to her about cats, you know, me owning Candy and all, to try and soften things up a bit. She told me not to speak of "un-academic-related subjects" during class. What seemed ironic to me was that *the bell had already rung and everybody was outside.*

"I am convinced," I insisted on the third Monday of school, "that woman *loathes* me."

"No, she doesn't," Penny replied with a wave of her hand. "All teachers love you because you're enthusiastic, cooperative, *blah blah blah*."

"Gee, thanks. That helps." I rolled my eyes.

"She has a point though," Olivia agreed. "I know your scholastic record in geography has lasted from . . . I don't know when! And I'm new!"

"Thanks, Liv," I sighed. "But how can you not notice? It's like she pretends I'm invisible."

"True." Elora used her straw to collect the last of her milkshake from the bottom of her cup as she spoke. "She does ignore your raised hand."

"*Thank you.*" I sighed. "Someone's noticing!"

"Okay, yes, she can be grumpy, but why do you think she's targeting *you* particularly?" Elora continued.

"Trust me, I can feel the hate waves coming towards me," I said with a frown as the bell rang. "What do we have now—*oh, man.*"

"What? I thought you loved geo!" Olivia raised an eyebrow as she pulled me up. We usually sat on the grass just outside the school building, under a rather small maple tree.

"I do, just not with her." I brushed the dust off my

33

pants. "Come on, I'll prove it to you."

And I did. The moment I walked in class she gave me a death stare that was sure to go right through me if she had laser eyes. I silently took my seat, hoping she'd just let go of me for one day.

The lesson began and Mrs. Kartley asked the opening question; "Which of you can tell me the common types of mountains? Anyone?"

I didn't even bother to raise my hand. I'd just drain the blood out of my arm uselessly.

"You should remember it from last year," she added, her eyebrows raised.

Nobody moved a muscle. I wasn't even tempted to answer so I sat there, staring out the window beside me and looking at Celestial Middle School from across campus, wondering what Maha was up to.

"Such a pity. Never have I met such an uncooperative class as you," she said as she turned to fix the presentation on the smartboard. Then she added, "Especially you, Meghan. I thought you were passionate about the study of the earth."

That smirk on her vile face made me want to rip her eyes out. That evil face that always had something for me.

Usually I was attentive and made the most of the period. This time though, I barely paid attention or did anything during class. The forty-five minutes flew by while I doodled in my scrapbook and thought of Mom at our day care, doing what she loves most and spending time with kids.

A few minutes before the bell rang, Mrs. Kartley handed out our essay homework and it didn't do me any good either.

After she gave Liv and Talia their essays (they sat in front of Lora and me), she stood by our desks and smiled at Elora.

"Fantastic job, Elora!" she congratulated as she handed her the sheets. "You should work on your sentence structure and sketches, but it's nevertheless fantastic!"

Elora took her paper, supremely excited. *"Ninety-six!"* she mouthed to me.

Then Mrs. Kartley turned her attention to me. I've never seen a teacher's face grow darker than now. She shook her head in disappointment. "You can do better, Baker."

Baker? She never called us by our last names. Correction: she never called *them* by their last name.

She handed me the sheet and seemed to float on evil as she glided to the table behind us.

I looked at the paper in my hands and a glum ninety-two looked up at me. *That's the lowest grade I've ever had in geography since sixth grade* . . . I felt panic rise inside me. I loved geo—no, I was *obsessed* with it. I spent my weekend working on it, and to me, the ninety-two was an understatement. I could've got an eighty-something in any other subject and I couldn't care less. But geography? It was different . . .

Anger bubbled up inside me. Elora seemed to notice because I felt her hand patting me gently on my back. I looked at her and met her smile. She scribbled something on a sticky note and passed it to me, an evil glint in her eye.

Leave her to me. >:)

I couldn't help smiling. Sure, Mrs. Kartley was sour, and mean, and unfair, but I was glad I had my friends with me.

Don't get yourself in trouble, young lady.

I scribbled and passed the note back. Elora snickered and nodded.

When the bell rang to signal the end of the period, Mrs. Kartley eyed me once more as she high-heeled out of the class.

"Did you *see* that?" Olivia turned around on her seat to

look at us. "She literally told Meg off for not raising her hand—which you always do and get *ignored*!"

"See?" I slumped down in my chair. "I did absolutely *nothing* to her, and all she gives me is *that look*." And I imitated the pitiful face she gave me whenever she ignored my raised hand.

The three of them laughed at the face I made. Penny came from across the room and raised an eyebrow. "What's so funny?"

"*You can do better, Baker.*" I mimicked Mrs. Kartley's face and mumbled under my breath, scrunching my nose in disgust, "*Meh, meh, meh, meh, meh.*"

Penny involuntarily laughed out loud and shook her head. "I'm sorry, I know I shouldn't be laughing about this, but your face is just *amazing*."

"Whatever," I shrugged as I leaned against the wall.

"Don't let her get to you," Liv smiled as she sat on my desk. "Just because she chose to be unpleasant, it shouldn't make you upset too."

"You know, Dad actually does that sometimes at college," Iris commented as she too joined us.

"What?" we simultaneously asked.

"Well, you know, him being a prof and all," she began explaining. "He says that sometimes he treats a student differently because he sees potential in them, you know, to push them to their limits. See their reactions. Stuff like that."

I thought about it in silence as the rest of the girls nodded in agreement. *It is kind of possible.*

"She still looks like she swallowed a lemon whole though," Elora added as she shuddered. "She can't stop shooting death stares at everybody."

"That's it!" Talia piped up. "That'll be our code name for her! Lemon Face!"

At that, the entire class was sent into fits of laughter.

"No, not that." She shook her head. "*Sour* face, to match her personality, too."

I couldn't help giggling a little as Talia smiled at me. "With that attitude, all she's ever going to be is stuck with her cats, alone in life, and *mean*."

The entire class erupted into a chorus of *Mean* by Taylor Swift as Mrs. Amena popped her head in from the doorway.

"Keep it down!" she hissed. "You're in high school now, no more of this middle school singing nonsense!"

Everybody fell silent before she smiled a little. "Just try and be a little quieter?"

"Sure will, Mrs. A," Penny smiled back before the vice principal left, leaving the class in a fit of giggles.

A not-so-long while later, chemistry commenced and

we were in the lab trying the "elephant toothpaste" experiment, whatever that was.

"We need a catalyst to speed up the reaction," Mrs. Evans continued explaining. "So what we're going to do is add—"

She was cut off mid-sentence as the lights flickered.

"*THE UPSIDE DOWN!*" Elora yelled, causing the class to go into a frenzy.

"Elora! Keep it down!" Mrs. Evans tried to calm the class as everybody was chattering excitedly. As if we weren't hyped enough, the lights went out and our screams were even louder.

"Nine-two! Please!" Mrs. Evans tried again. "There's no need to yell; it's just a power outage!"

"It's mandatory," I smirked. "Just like a reflex. We have to scream when the lights go out, because that means a few more minutes of fun and a few dozen more wasted minutes of class."

"*Excuse me?*" She raised an eyebrow.

"Nothing." I stifled a giggle as Elora poked me in the ribs and Penny widened her eyes at me.

The entire class headed outside without waiting for permission, all other classes apparently doing the same. The warm sun showered us with light as cheers filled the lawn.

"How does this feel after the geo-fiasco?" Elora asked

me as she side-hugged me.

"Okay," I half-smiled. I couldn't shake that subdued feeling in the pit of my stomach.

"Come on." She nudged me. "Don't let her get to you. Just . . . let go of it, chill out a little. Ignore what bothers you from her. It'll be better for you. Don't let her—or anyone— ruin your mood because of their lousy behavior. Or, as I read in a book once, *be proactive."*

5 TIME-EXPLORER 3000

The once-plain purple walls of Celestial High were now covered in all sorts of posters—encouraging flyers, after-school clubs, this term's matches, and suggestion forms for this year's play; just about everything.

I spent all the way home discussing the gazillion after-school clubs with Elora. We took our usual path, the only difference being Maha was not with us (her best friend's mom picked them up).

"What would you want with a *martial arts* club, seriously?" I argued.

"Imagine how cool it'd be to karate-chop stuff right outta my dad's hands!" Elora replied as she imitated some random karate moves while walking.

"Yeah, I get it, it's cool and all, but it's not worth wasting forty-five minutes—three times a week."

"Says the girl who wants to join the robot club." She nudged me.

"Yeah, I could help Mike invent stuff."

"Exactly! You don't *need* a club—you have an older brother for that."

She suddenly came to a halt as her eyes widened.

"Elora, what is it?" I asked suspiciously.

Her lips curved into a huge smile as she began hopping up and down and clapping her hands together.

"What if we joined the *drama club*?"

"We were in the play last year, remember?"

"Yeah, but that was a middle school play. I want to take acting seriously."

Elora has had her mind set on becoming an actress since fifth grade. Ever since, she's participated in every play possible; around town or in school, not to mention a photoshoot for a local department store.

"Okay, that sounds cool," I nodded as we resumed talking. "But I'll only go along with it for you."

"What if you joined the young geographers' club?" Her tone was getting more excited by the second. "Their meetings are held on the same days—at the same times!" she said, pointing to the schedule she had in her hand.

"Sounds good to me!" I agreed as I unlocked the front

door. The fresh smell of brownies welcomed my nostrils.

"Oooh, who's baking?" I asked the empty house.

Usually, I was the first home. Mom would be at her day care (yes, she founded it) two blocks away, unless one of her employees could fill in. Dad was at work, and Michael arrives shortly after I do.

"Hello!" Michael's head appeared from around the kitchen doorframe. "I have baked these delicious brownies!"

"What did you invent?" Elora asked as she tossed her backpack on the couch and sank beside it.

Everybody knew Michael only baked when he's made *a groundbreaking discovery*—his words, not mine.

"I, my dear friends, have . . ." He looked from my face to Elora's to build up the suspense. "Why don't I just show you?"

We followed him up the stairs and into the attic. Two white mice squeaked in welcome from their cages, sniffling about.

"Last lecture was cancelled, so I thought I'd come home to finish up this baby—and I did!"

He switched on a button from somewhere and the iron lump illuminated with blue light. The seat, circle, and everything around it had blue LEDs attached, which gave it that futuristic glow I bet Michael was aiming for.

"What do you think?" he asked eagerly.

"What do *I* think?" Elora looked at the Time Explorer 3000 in disbelief. "I think you're a *genius*!"

"Yeah, but why'd you finish it without me?" I asked with a fake pout.

"I wanted to surprise you," he laughed. "Anyway, who wants to see it in action? I've tried it a few times, and let me tell you, *it is slick*."

He gently took one of the snowy mice from its cage and settled it on another cage on the seat. He firmly set it in place with a seat belt he applied and passed us safety goggles.

"Why? Is it gonna blast some sort of radiation?" I asked as I slipped them on.

"Nope. For cool measures, you know," he smirked, and motioned for us to step back. He dialed some numbers on the keypad next to the seat and stepped back.

"Ladies, I present to you, *time travel*." He pressed a button on a remote he was holding.

Blue lightning came out of the donut-metal thingy and circled itself. The ring began spinning wildly around the chair in the middle and in a split-second it began slowing down; the chair was gone.

"Michael! My goodness, you're brilliant!" I looked from the machine to him and back at the machine. Elora looked just as awestruck as I did.

Mike wasn't any less enthusiastic about it, either. He

was recording notes on a large notepad and monitoring a stopwatch.

"But how will he get back?" Elora asked, visibly worried about the mouse.

"I set a timer to bring him back," Michael explained. "Didn't you notice the chair's gone? I set a timer for two minutes. When the time's up, the chair will return, carrying whoever is on it with it."

Soon enough, the ring began rapidly spinning once more, the chair fading into focus. It gradually slowed down, the mouse's cage appearing with it.

Michael hurried forward and checked a few things before removing the cage.

"Brilliant. Mickey's not affected! He's not even dizzy!"

I guess he named them, too.

"The departure takes about ten seconds, which is normal, taking the object's weight into account . . ."

I felt so proud of him. He'd been working on time travel for over three years now, and to see him finally accomplish it, I felt very happy—almost as happy as he was!

"How do you know it goes to the future, anyway?" Elora asked, still bewildered by what she had just witnessed.

"Didn't you notice there's cheese inside the cage now?" he began. "It wasn't there when I sent him."

"Future you put it there?" I completed the thought for him.

"Precisely. I only sent him to next Saturday, between 10:00 and 11:00 AM. I planned to sit there and observe next Saturday, which I probably did, seeing there's cheese in there."

"Genius," I whispered to myself. "Simply awesome."

"Go ahead, you can crown me king scientist now," he said, an overly excited look on his face. "*I CRACKED TIME TRAVEL!*" he yelled at the top of his lungs and began dancing around. "*I CAN'T WAIT TO TELL DAD!*"

I couldn't help but laugh. Of course, I was proud as any sister could be, but I still laughed. It was a funny scene.

Elora and I spent the remainder of our time playing the Game of Life and tackled a bit of our homework together. She asked her mom to stay so she could see how my folks would react.

Around sunset, when we'd all had our dinner, Michael gathered us upstairs and crammed us into his lab (I am forbidden to say "attic," since he was the first to crack time travel, and now it's his "lair"). He gave us all goggles to wear and demonstrated once more what we saw that afternoon, Elora documenting everything.

"Wonderful, Mike, wonderful!" Dad was ecstatic. He wanted to know everything and went on about how his son could and would change the world.

Mom cried. She cried because she couldn't believe it. She cried because she was so proud. She cried because her own son just accomplished what people have attempted for *decades*.

Maha was even more crazed. She went on about how Michael was "an absolutely awesome big brother."

I was speechless. It was crazy. My own *brother* had the ability to travel through time. I couldn't believe it. Simply, *wow*.

"The thing is, I need a human test subject." He cut through the excitement, a little bit of nervousness on his face. "I mean, it only travels a few weeks, as far as I know, but I can't be sure this works until a human goes in."

The entire room went silent. No one was willing to risk something as huge as this.

"Nobody?" I saw the color and happiness of a few moments before draining out of his face. It made me feel sad. Really sad. I felt bad for him. Just one last step and he'd be making history . . .

"It's okay." He turned away. I could feel his disappointment. "I could put up a volunteering sheet on campus for people who wouldn't mind experiments run on them. Maybe in town hall . . ."

"I'll do it."

The entire room swiveled towards me.

"Meghan, are you *mental*?" Elora's eyes grew wider than tennis balls.

"Meg?" Dad looked at me in disbelief.

"No, I won't allow this." Mom shook her head, determination in her eyes. She looked fierce.

"I say we send our neighbor's dog!" Maha shrugged. "Just kidding." She shrank at the look Mom gave her.

"I'm serious." I was serious. I *am* serious. "Mike worked hard for this, and victory is just a hop, skip, and a jump ahead. Why not send me? Just for next Saturday."

Michael's face lit up. The energy and enthusiasm flooded into it once again. I would've done anything to see him happy again. After all he's done for me, it was the least I can do.

Mom shook her head in disbelief, speechless. "That's a hop, skip, and a jump I'm not willing to attempt, Meghan."

"What if you get stuck in the future?" Dad protested.

"It's only next Saturday. You'll see me then."

"What will we tell the school?"

"Tell them I was sick."

"What if—"

"Dad, just give me a chance." I put my hand on his shoulder, smiling. "Give Mike a chance. If mice can do it, so can I."

He sighed heavily as he looked from Mike's expectant face to my reassuring one.

"Fine."

Mike prepared the seat as fast as he could, set up monitors *everywhere*, and went about preparing notepads for what felt like ten minutes.

"Come on." He motioned for me to take a seat. That's when reality kicked in.

Meghan, you're going to travel through time. This is no ordinary road trip. You're gonna defy all laws of physics ever and see next week right now. Why did you volunteer to do this?

What if I split in two? What if I get stuck in a second permanently? What if I . . . I died?

All these thoughts kept swimming in my head as he sat me down and tightened the seat belt around me. I guess he felt my pulse because he looked me in the eyes and smiled.

"You're gonna be fine."

"I'm scared," I whispered, careful about Mom not hearing. She was already arguing with Dad about, "*How on earth could you let your own daughter do this?!*"

"You'll be all right, I promise," he assured me. "The worst that could happen is a minor electric shock, nothing more."

I took a deep breath and looked at Mom, Dad, Maha, and Elora facing me. Mom was hiding her face.

"I'll see you guys in a couple of minutes!" I chirped as the ring began spinning around me. Around and around the metal spun, until it became a haze of blue and silver. I closed my eyes to avoid dizziness, kept my limbs the closest I could to me and took deep breaths, holding onto the handrests as hard as I could.

As I felt the wind around me ease, I opened my eyes to see Mike's lab coming into view—except it wasn't sundown. It was—*morning?* As the machine came to a halt, I saw a bewildered Mike, Elora, Dad, Candy, and—*me?*

There I stood, in my own flesh and blood, staring at myself.

"Oh my God," future me breathed, her amazed expression meeting mine.

"It *did* work!" future Elora exclaimed as she walked towards me. "Can I touch you or will that be creepy?"

"Go ahead." I was shocked. Future Elora touched my face and screamed, "*It's really real!*"

Future Mike and Meg ran up and started investigating me. I was too stunned for words.

"What did I get on my vocabulary test?" I couldn't help asking.

"Eight out of ten," future me immediately replied, still freaked out. Oh well, I was never any good in English. I bet I was gonna find out how being this freaked-out felt—in a few days.

I looked at the timer on my chair—twenty-six seconds till going back.

"Guys, the chair goes back in less than twenty seconds. So, uh, you might wanna step back." The panic must've been obvious in my voice because they—we—UGH—future us sprang back as I felt the chair vibrate once more.

I felt the wind around me, but couldn't see where the donut (yes, I'm calling it donut from now on) was.

I could see the sunset-flooded room again—quite fuzzy—but it was there. I felt the wind slow down, but it picked up speed again. I saw the morning-lit room again. On and off. Sunset, morning, sunset, morning. I saw flashes between Monday and Saturday, unsure where time would be taking me.

The chair started shaking violently. I felt dizzy as the wind picked up and slowed down, on and off. In the future, they—*we*—were calm and just . . . watching me.

Present them were panicking—I think. It was blurry, but I think I saw Mom frantically holding Elora for support. Dad . . . helping Mike? Tackling wires or something? I was scared. *Deathly* afraid.

I didn't want Mom and Dad to get mad at Mike, so I fought the strong urge to yell. I felt the wind against me, my fingers clinging onto the seat for dear life.

The last thing I saw was Dad tugging at some wires and calling my name . . .

And then I blacked out.

6 IT'S MY FAULT

I had no idea how long I'd been out for. I felt soft fabric against my arms and a cold sensation against my forehead and cheeks.

I tried to open my eyelids, but they felt heavy. I opened them a small crack and saw a soft, white light silhouetting a person. Probably a woman, judging by her long hair.

I opened my eyes fully and saw about six women huddled around me. No, eight, actually. No, four. *Seven?* Whatever.

I closed my eyes again and enjoyed the darkness. I felt too tired to move a muscle. I couldn't stop the stupid question that escaped my lips:

"Am I . . . *dead?*"

I recognized a familiar laugh, one I always heard when I

made a lame pun.

"Yes, you're dead, and I'm your guardian angel here to pick you up so we can go to heaven. Wanna carpool with a few other dead bodies?"

I recognized that voice, too. One I heard every day.

"*MRS. SUSAN*!" Elora yelled. "*MEG'S CONSCIOUS*!"

I winced at the loud sound. "Please keep it down, I can't take it."

I opened my eyes to see Mom rush in, her face a blob of brown and rose. She ran up to me and hugged me like she never had before.

"I knew this was a bad idea," she began babbling, me still in her arms. "I kept silent because your dad agreed and I didn't want to ruin Mike's excitement, but my guts told me it was a bad idea. My heart stopped when I saw you disappear, when the thing began shaking I almost fainted, but when I saw you unconscious, fallen out of that . . . that *monstrosity*, I was going to die.

"Meghan, please, *please*, never, ever, *ever* do this again. It was horrible. I understand it's his life's dream and all but he's not doing it on you ever again. On any of us. He can find volunteers all he wants around town, but I'm not risking any of my children, no way. I was going to take you to the ER but they said it was unnecessary. If you hadn't woken up soon I was gonna drive you there myself."

She stopped and inhaled deeply. "I'm just glad you're okay."

I felt a tear wet my forehead.

"Now you lay back down, sweetie. You need all the rest you can get."

I printed a kiss on her forehead as I set my head back on the pillow. I noticed again how really tired I was. And worn-out.

I saw Mom's face transform from "worried-and-tired rose" to "somebody's-gonna-regret-something" scarlet.

"I will *show* that *Michael*. He doesn't even *worry* about his sister! So *carelessly* agreeing to let his own *little* sister go on such a *dangerous* trek!"

"Mom, don't—" I sat bolt upright, making myself wince once more.

"*MICHAEL TIMOTHY BAKER, YOU COME HERE THIS INSTANT!*" she bellowed. I had to cover my ears from how loud she was. My wince was more of a full-body shake. I still heard her voice ringing in my ears when I heard the thud-thud upstairs of feet running to the living room.

Michael skidded to a halt in front of the living room, his eyes puffy and red, his face covered with shame.

"Oh, thank goodness!" He ran up to me and hugged me tightly. "You're all right."

"*Michael, you're in so much trouble, young man.* How *dare* you put your sister in such danger!" Mom's eyes looked as menacing as ever. Elora slipped out of the room.

"Mom, I—" he began.

"Don't you *dare* Mom me. Your sister almost *died*. An electric shock that knocked her *unconscious*! Why would you let her go in just like that?"

"Dad said—"

"I *don't* care what your father said. You made a terrible, *lethal* mistake. You should've told him no. This is all *your* fault. If there are any side effects, *anything* wrong with Meghan, it'll be all your fault!"

I saw his eyes fill up with tears as he fought to hold them back.

"You're *forbidden* to go near that lab for two weeks, do you hear? No science experiments or any of these shenanigans for . . . a month, actually. *Two months.*"

I saw Michael's face drain of color. Science was his future; his everything. He loved it more than anything else. I hated to see all of that taken away from him, his entire career and favorite hobby.

"Mom, that's unfair," I interrupted her. She aimed her death stare at me.

"*Explain why your opinion matters here.*" Her face was menacing; I regretted saying that immediately.

"Uh, because . . ." I searched my mind for an excuse, *any excuse.* "It's not his fault the time traveler malfunctioned."

"It's not?"

"No."

"*Explain.*"

"Because, I uh, messed with . . . the controls . . . in the future." The lie felt heavy on my tongue.

"You *what?*" they replied in unison.

"The keypad on the armrest," I explained, hating myself for telling such a lie. "I saw a few buttons and wanted to find out what it'd do. The machine was doing fine until I tampered with it."

"Meghan, *why?*" Mom's eyes were full of concern now. "*Anything* could've happened. *Don't* disobey instructions, I've told you a *million* times!"

"I'm sorry." My face burned red with shame. "I won't mess with what I don't understand again."

"We're lucky you came back in one piece," she sighed as she hugged me again.

She turned to Mike. His face was startled.

"Mike, I—"

"No, Mom, you're right. I should've been more careful with my calculations. Maybe the machine wasn't ready to accommodate humans yet."

Mom sighed heavily after a painfully long silence. "Everyone makes mistakes. Meghan, don't *ever* tamper with stuff that you don't understand. And Mike." She looked at him. "You can keep working in the lab just fine. It needs tidying up anyway."

My mind went back to the Time Explorer 3000. I let out an audible gasp.

"What happened to the Time Explorer?" I jumped off the sofa.

"*Sit back down*, Meghan," Mom said as she pulled me back. "You need rest."

"But what about the time machine?"

"It's okay."

"Did anything happen to it?"

"It's perfectly fine," Mike assured me, finally speaking. "Just a few uninstalled wires, that's all."

I let Mom push me back down as I felt the pain in my head multiply.

"Dang it, my research paper." I remembered all the homework I had to turn in.

"Forget it. I'm telling the school you're sick. No way you're going in a state like this," Mom prompted.

"What if my friends ask? What should I say?"

"Sick."

I sighed. A day off school was always a blast, especially when tomorrow was a Wednesday—mid-week break. Then why was I so deflated?

"Have some time off, sweetie. I'll go get you something to eat." Mom kissed me on my forehead as she and Mike walked out.

Mike stopped at the doorway and smiled at me; his hair still crazy, his eyes still reddened. I smiled back. Maybe a weak smile, but it was still a smile. And he walked away.

As I rubbed my forehead to soothe the pain, I noticed a scar on my left forearm. I bolted upright, unable to believe my eyes. It was *silver*. Silver with streaks of neon blue. Just about three centimeters long and half a centimeter wide. Still cool.

I was tracing it with my finger when Elora slipped in.

"I heard the convo. Did you really mess with—*what is that?*" She rushed over and squeezed herself onto the sofa beside me as she grabbed my arm to have a closer look.

"*Ow!* Be careful."

The scar beautifully reflected the soft white light. I felt her cold finger run against it.

"This is awesome," she breathed. "*Warrior scar!*"

I laughed. "What do you think caused it, though?"

"Maybe you splinched?" She narrowed her eyes to see clearer. "I dunno. Some inter-dimensional time crack or something."

I looked at the silvery-blue etching. Was it supposed to be painful? Was I an idiot to think it was pretty?

Mom walked in with some oatmeal and a warm cup of—deep breath—*coffee*.

"What on earth happened to your arm?" Mom hastily set the tray on the coffee table (how ironic) as soon as she saw my arm. I felt her grip tighten around my forearm. *Wince*.

"It's okay, I don't feel anything." I didn't want her overthinking it, and I certainly didn't want to get Michael into more trouble.

"It's numb?"

"No, no, no, I mean, it isn't painful or anything. Probably just a scratch."

"Maybe." She sat on the footrest and gave me the bowl of oatmeal. "Eat up." And walked out.

"What are we gonna tell everyone in class?" Elora whispered urgently.

"Uh . . . sick?"

"You're unbelievable." She shook her head. "Well, I'd better get going. It's a school night, after all. Mom will kill me. It's deadly late and I begged her to let me stay until you woke up."

"*Deadly late*? What time is it?"

"Around midnight. Yeah, you were out for quite a while," she answered my bewildered face. "I'm glad you're okay."

"I'm glad you're here." I smiled. "Thanks, by the way. And why was it your face I saw first?"

"Because you need someone to give an awesome answer to your stupid *am I dead* question. Besides, I wasn't gonna leave until I made sure you were okay."

"Thanks." I hugged her. "Aren't you the best?"

"I'm called your best friend for a reason."

"Come to think of it, *I'm* glad I survived it. Don't tell Mom, but I was *so scared* I almost yelled."

"I knew you were, it was written all over your face."

"Do you think Mom noticed?"

"She had her eyes closed."

"Figures."

After she left, she popped her head back in. "You survived middle school; I expected you to survive *this*."

7 WARRIOR SCAR

I slept until around 3:00 PM the next day. I had no idea time traveling wore you out so much. Again, Elora's face was the first thing I saw.

"Rise 'n' shine, Meg!" She was on her phone, spinning in my desk chair as her auburn curls went flying in every direction. I sat on the edge of my bed, remembering what had happened last night.

I was looking at Elora spinning when the chair abruptly stopped spinning. She was even wearing a different outfit . . . I probably just didn't see her clearly.

"What color nails would you like?" she asked.

"I was thinking something purple and blue," I found myself involuntarily replying. I held out my nails for her to see.

"Well then, let me bedazzle your cuticles!" She jazz-handed me and sprang to my vanity, where she opened my nail care drawer and rummaged through it.

"Don't mess anything up!" I warned her.

But then I . . . I don't know. I looked at Elora, and she was sitting in my desk chair, raising an eyebrow. Her clothes were different.

"Uh, hello? I asked you a question here."

I stared at her blankly. "What?"

"I said how do you feel, and all you did was stare at me blankly."

"I, uh, feel fine. A lot less tired." I thought about this for a while. What *did* just happen? Was I just hallucinating? And why on earth was it so *strong*?

I set that thought aside as she caught me up on what I missed. Apparently, Elora told *everyone* in our class I was absent because of a "lab accident."

"*Why'd you say that*? Mom will kill me!"

"Duh, so we can have a believable excuse for your warrior scar—yes, that's what I'm calling it—and then tomorrow, *you* explain what the supposed accident was."

"Like what?"

"I don't know, chemical spill or Bunsen burner burn, just figure something out."

"You didn't tell anyone he cracked time travel?"

"Nope. Your mom told me to keep it between us. I'm not even allowed to tell my family."

She spent her time with me for the remainder of the afternoon and helped me do a little bit of my work. Stayed until sunset.

"You know you're the best, right?" I called after her as I waved from our house's doorway.

"*Ugh*, so you keep saying that," she smiled as she walked backwards on her front lawn.

I walked back in after I saw her get inside and had dinner with my own family. Bakers minus one.

Once I swallowed the last bite of lasagna, I excused myself for "needing rest" and took the stairs two at a time. Mike wasn't in his room. Not that I expected him to be there.

I went up the stairs leading to the attic (Dad upgraded them to ease our way up and down) and saw the back of my big brother.

I knew he was crying yesterday. Of course, I wasn't gonna say it to his face. I felt guilty for causing all this trouble. Mom was having limited conversations with him. He obviously felt guilty about almost harming me. I had to make things right.

"Hey, Dr. Michaelstein."

I caught him off guard. He jumped out of his skin as he turned to face me. Oh no, his eyes were still red. What had I done?

"Hey, Meg." He smiled and put down the papers in his hands to help me up.

"How's tidying up coming along?"

The room itself answered me. There were still a few bits and pieces, papers, tools and other unidentified objects sprawled on the floor. Most things were neatly on the shelves though.

And then my eyes met the Time Explorer. It was terrible. All the wires that were once plugged in were all over the place; some unplugged, others just fried.

The chair was out of place. He had removed it and instead there sat withered pieces of metal. But that wasn't the worst.

The left side of the ring was totally ruined. It was black; a saddening black that surrounded a part missing; a part blasted off.

It was a miserable view. All his arduous work, gone. I imagined how heartbroken he must've been. Almost a year tinkering; a year of research and fixing details. It was horrible, standing there, watching everything fade away.

"Mike, I . . ." I didn't know what to say. "I'm sorry. I didn't mean for this to happen."

"It wasn't your fault," he sadly replied. "I didn't make sure it could handle human transport."

He stopped and looked me in the eyes. "You didn't tamper with anything."

I fell silent for a moment. *Should I just come clean? Or play on for a bit?*

Finally, I replied, "How'd you find out?"

"I have a history on this thing. The hardware's fried but the software is still in perfect shape." He sighed heavily and continued picking fallen debris from the floor, so I bent down to help him. Turned out they were exploded pieces of the Time Explorer's ring. My heart ached with every piece I picked up. His entire life had been leading to this moment; now it was gone.

"Come on." I got up and pulled him with me.

"Wait, I need to finish cleaning up!"

"It can wait."

I dragged him behind me as I went to my bedroom and slid the window open.

"Follow me."

I climbed out and made my way sideways until I reached the roof and motioned for him to follow me.

As he hesitated, I took a seat and patted a space next to me. He took off his lab coat and came clambering out. I helped him up and we took a seat beside each other, the sky painted a purplish-red.

"Why'd we come here?" he asked.

"I come here a lot, usually to think. Sometimes I just like being left alone for a while."

"How are you not afraid of falling?"

"It's not that steep."

We stayed in silence; both of us staring at the horizon, the cool, September breeze against our faces.

"Why did you lie?" he finally asked.

"When?"

"You didn't mess with the controls."

I fell silent. What was I supposed to say? That I felt guilty? That I felt it was unfair? That I wanted to save him?

"I don't know, it seemed right."

"*How?*"

Another silence.

"Mom was furious. She was in a state of shock and total confusion. You did nothing wrong. It's just a failed attempt at a science experiment, and I'm okay."

He buried his face in his hands and sighed heavily.

"If anything happened to you, I wouldn't have forgiven myself," he began, his voice breaking. "Mom was right. This *is* all my fault."

"No, it wasn't. You and I both know she didn't mean what she said. She was just . . . disturbed, that's all."

I sat and thought about my scar. Something had happened, but it was no big deal. Apparently, Mom hadn't told anybody about it.

I looked at his sad figure.

Then the sky suddenly went from fiery blue to bright yellow, like sometime in the cool afternoons of September.

I was wearing my favorite purple, long-sleeved t-shirt and smirked at him.

"Come on, Maha told me everything," he urged.

"Fine, but don't feel bad, okay?"

"I *promise*, I'm over that. You're in decent shape. I just need to see it to analyze what my baby can do!"

I gave him the evilest smile I could muster. "Do you think you're ready?"

"Just show me!"

I pulled up my left sleeve and flashed him my silver-blue beauty. "How's *that* for cool measure?"

"Oh, my God," he whispered. "This is incredible! I need a sample and details when we get down, deal?"

"You've got yourself a deal, Dr. Michaelstein," I said as

I pulled my sleeve back down and firmly shook his hand.

And then the world was sunset-y again. *What* just happened? I looked at Michael, but his face was still in his hands. Okay, so this didn't really happen. Was I beginning to hallucinate a lot? Did the accident affect me? Were these delusions a side effect?

"But what if something *did* happen." He startled me as he suddenly spoke. "How foolish would *that* have been?"

"Nothing *did* happen. Stop thinking about the ifs and focus on what's really happening. I'm okay; there's no reason for you to feel guilty." I pushed my worries to the back of my brain. Mike was more important.

"I can't help it. I keep thinking . . . what I would've done with myself if something had happened. What would I do then?" He looked at me, his face as tired as ever. "Maybe experimenting shouldn't be my thing."

"No, I will not stand for this." I looked at him seriously and leveled my eyes with his. "I didn't lie so you can give up. Michael, you are a *genius* in the lab. You truly are. A simple bump in the road shouldn't cause you to abandon that course completely. You are great at what you do; don't let anybody change that."

He covered his face in his hands again. I had to bring him out of this funk.

"Look at me. You cracked *time travel*, something scientists have been trying to do for years. *Actual time travel.*

And that is why I brought you here in the first place. You are a *legend*, whether the world knows it or not. Don't feel guilty about me."

I stopped for breath and looked at the horizon once again.

"I'm sorry about the machine. I promise, I'll help fix it every day."

He looked at me, a small smile on his face. "That'll have to do, I guess."

I couldn't help laughing. "Mike, listen. I'm serious. I feel bad about this entire situation and if I'm the reason you decide to quit, I'm going to feel guilty about it for the rest of my life."

"You know, you're a great sister," he said as he pulled me into a side-hug. "Don't feel bad; I'm still Dr. Michaelstein."

And that's when I knew everything was gonna be okay.

***

The next day at school, everybody was crazed by my "warrior scar." The name caught on, and *everyone* from both buildings found out.

Elora was right; I was asked over and over what the accident was. I chose "chemical malfunction" as the subtlest reply.

Apparently, Ms. Avery found out too. Today when she

walked in, the first thing she did was motion for me to come to the front of the class.

"What did I do?" I asked at first.

"Just come."

She took my forearm between her hands and touched it. I could see the impressed look in her eyes.

"*Warrior scar*, huh?" she commented. "Sweet."

The same went for every teacher. Each one of them was interested in what and how this happened.

Mrs. Kartley, of course, was as interested in my scar as I was in politics. I'll give you the answer: zero percent.

I caught her trying to sneak a look, so I thought I'd give her a peek.

"Now, can anyone tell me the Alps' length?" She scanned the class for volunteers.

I raised my *left* arm, for her to see the warrior scar everyone was talking about.

"Yes, Baker?"

"What?" I was caught off guard.

"Didn't you raise your hand to answer?"

"Uh, yes, I did." My mind went blank as I lowered my hand in shame. I forgot what the question was.

"Yes, I think," I improvised as I looked at the

smartboard. The Alps, yeah, that's what she asked. "The Alps stretch for 1,200 kilometers, with Mont Blanc as its highest point, dominating most of Central Europe."

"Well worded."

The entire class was awed. Elora looked at me with a surprised smile and Liv shot me a thumbs up. Okay, Sour Face was still sour, but at least I *finally* got to answer.

I gave no details of the so-called chemical spill to anyone out of my close friends circle. Didn't want the entire school to know that I have a silvery-blue scar because of my older brother.

"Lemme see, LEMME SEE!" Talia almost screamed during lunchtime.

"Okay, okay, calm down." I pulled up my hoodie sleeve and handed her my, well, hand.

Olivia, Penny, Talia, Elora, and I sat under our usual maple tree right outside the school building, all eyes on us— well, *me*. As I was scanning the yard, I saw Liz with a bunch of her friends.

"Be right back." I got up and kind of jogged over to her. "Hey, Liz!"

"Meghan! Hey!" She turned and left her friends talking. "How's it going?"

"Great! I was just wondering, we sign up for the after-school clubs through you, right?"

"Yep! What are you signing up for?"

"Meghan Baker for the Junior Geographers and Elora Black for the Juvenile Theatre."

"Sure thing," she replied as she got her clipboard seemingly out of nowhere and wrote it down. "Hey, I hope I'm not interfering or anything, but are the rumors real?"

"Which rumors?"

"You know, the 'warrior scar' and all." She made air quotation marks with her fingers.

"As real as it'll ever be," I smiled, as I once more subtly pulled up my sleeve.

"Whoa. Can I touch it?" She seemed kind of hesitant and shy to ask that.

"Of course! Be careful though, it might give you an electric shock." Her eyes widened as she stopped. She was the eleventh person to fall for it today. "Just kidding!"

"A lab accident?"

"Yep."

"Cool. Anyway, I'll notify the heads of the clubs and update you later, okay?"

"Thanks!"

As I walked back to my friends, more people were staring. It felt weirdly awesome. *Meghan, the girl with the Warrior Scar.* How cool was that? I was a celebrity for a day.

8 DÉJÀ VU

I kept having those weird hallucinations throughout the next couple of days—and may I say, at the *worst* times possible. I almost got told off by Ms. Avery, and Dad *did* get annoyed as I spaced out while he was talking.

"You'll be getting more interrogations," Elora began as we turned right on the street and left school for the weekend. I had just finished talking to a middle-schooler who—you guessed it—was dared by her friends to ask me about my scar. "You're almost as popular as when we were chosen to play Queen Anne and Duchess Teresa."

"Yeah, but it's getting creepy," I admitted. "Them touching my arm and just—" I shuddered and gagged to demonstrate how I felt. "Even wearing long sleeves doesn't help."

"Oh, you wait and see." She waved her hand

dismissively. "Something else will come up and it'll all blow over. Trust me, *Sarah, the drama-queen, attention-loving persona,* will make sure of that."

My laugh made a few other people walking turn to look at me. "Did you *see* her face when Mrs. Evans asked to see it?"

"Her eyes almost fell *out of her head*."

"I guess she doesn't enjoy not being the topic of every conversation."

"She's been the talk of the school since she bought that iPhone prototype or something. Must be pretty jealous you got the attention."

"The only thing I'm enjoying about this is it'll wipe that smile off her face. It's only her first year here and she acts like the queen of the school. Riley says she needs a knock upside her head to set her straight."

"Who's Riley?"

Oh, right. Riley. It *might* have slipped my mind to mention her.

"Oh, just a cousin of mine. We met at that wedding during summer; the one I told you about."

"Anyway," she changed the subject, that glow she had in her eyes making an appearance, one that showed up when she talked about something she loves. "I was at the mall yesterday when I saw the best thing ever."

"A Magcon poster?"

"I wish, but this was even *better.*"

"I'm all ears."

"I overheard two people talking,"

"Eavesdropping? Elora Meredith Black, I thought you were better than this."

"No! Just listen. So, I heard them talking about this huge, new movie that's being planned, and there are auditions in a few weeks. You know, no biggie."

"Elora! A *movie role*? This is amazing! They won't know what hit them."

"But that's not the best part." Her smile widened as she said so. "You won't *believe* who it's starring."

"Jennifer Lawrence?"

"*YES!*"

"Are you serious?"

"Dead serious!"

I dare anyone who saw us to state a scene that was more embarrassing; we were squealing and jumping up and down on the sidewalk in front of a grocery store.

"You get to be in a movie with *the* Jennifer Lawrence? Who are you auditioning for?" I was really happy. One of us was going to make her dream come true early; to me, one of us meant both of us.

"I don't know yet, but I found a complete website online," she explained, her voice not a bit less enthusiastic.

"Tell me more," I insisted as we stopped at a pedestrian red light.

Then suddenly the sky transformed into a navy blue, enveloping the world in its night.

". . . I was nervous at first, but I think I did pretty well. The director seemed impressed," Elora was saying. We were walking down that same street, but still weren't at the crosswalk yet.

"I think I got the part though. They asked me for my phone number and email before I left. Then again, they might do that for every auditionee."

Elora was talking half to herself as I rubbed my hands together inside my hoodie's pocket, lost in my thoughts. I stopped at the crosswalk but Elora kept walking.

"Lora! It's a red light for us!" I called after her.

"What?"

I motioned for her to come.

"The street's empty, *come on*." She turned on her heel and kept walking.

"Lora, come on, rules are—" But it all happened in slow motion after that.

A car rounded the corner and was speeding towards us, apparently unaware of the two girls ahead.

"*ELORA!*" I yelled after her, panic rising inside me.

She stopped midway and glared. "What now?"

I looked at the vehicle barreling towards us and back at my best friend. For some reason, I found myself jumping in the middle of the road, aiming to shove her out of the car's way.

The last thing that happened was bright headlights blinding me and deafening, screeching wheels before I snapped back to reality.

"Hello? Meghan, you're not even listening!"

I looked at Elora and back at the street. It was morning again and she was standing beside me, the pedestrian light still red.

I breathed heavily as I looked from her to the street and back to her, my heart rate crazy.

"Are you okay?" I finally managed to say.

"No, because you're *not listening*! What is up with you these days?"

I looked at the street, but there was no sign of any car, just an old couple sitting on a bench across the street.

"Is there something you're hiding from me?" she asked me as the light turned green and we began walking.

"No." What was there to say? That I'm having weird hallucinations several times a day that feel very real?

"Are you sure?" She looked at me, her face somewhere between doubt and concern.

"Yeah, I'm fine."

"You've been distracted a lot lately. What is it?"

"Just a bit dazed." I shook it off. "Anyway, you were saying?"

"Nothing."

We remained in an uncomfortable silence for a couple of minutes. It was never hard to talk to Lora. Why was it difficult now?

"Our after-school activities begin next week." I finally thought of something to break the silence.

"Yeah, Liz told me," she mumbled.

Cue another few awkward minutes.

"What happened to your nails?" she suddenly asked.

"Oh, the polish started peeling so I removed it altogether. I was meaning to redo my nails soon but—"

"You forgot. Typical Meg. Come on, I saw this really cute nail tutorial on Instagram last night that I want to try."

She pulled my hand and we broke into a run. My house appeared seconds later and we barged into the living room, grateful for the warmth.

"You never really feel the cold until you're warm," she commented as we ran upstairs and tossed our bags onto my bed.

"Tell me, what did it look like?" I began as I took off my jacket and sat cross-legged on the edge of my bed.

"It had a kind of color bubbles, but with lines and— you'll see." She sat on my desk chair and began scrolling through her phone. "There it is!" She turned her phone around to show me. "Okay, so we need a base color. How long are your nails again? And what color nails would you like?" she asked.

"I was thinking something purple and blue," I said as I held out my nails for her to see.

"Well then, let me bedazzle your cuticles!" She jazz-handed me and sprang to my vanity, where she opened my nail care drawer and rummaged through it.

"Don't mess anything up!" I warned her.

"I won't," she said as she took a bottle, inspected it, and either put it back or tossed it to me.

That's when I remembered Wednesday. Maybe that strong hallucination wasn't a hallucination. Probably just . . . a strong déjà vu?

Back then, it felt like I was living it. The sensation I had right now was exactly what I felt a few days ago.

"Okay, how do you feel about Passionate Purple?" she asked as she sat beside me and showed me a pretty purple polish I'd never seen before.

"I never bought that." I racked my brain to remember when and if someone gave this to me.

"No, I did. It matches the design in my brain perfectly. Now, give me your hands please."

"Meghan?" I heard Michael open the front door and walk in. "Are you home?"

"Upstairs!" I called back as Elora began arranging the colorful polish bottles on my bedside table.

A short while later he appeared at my door, a smile on his face. "How was school?"

"What's happening?" I hated when he wore that smile. It meant he had something for me—both good and/or bad. Last time he had that smile, it ended up with me getting all his chores for two weeks.

"What are you girls doing?"

"Getting ready to bedazzle our nails," Elora replied, still busy with the polish.

"I hope I won't disturb you, but I have a visitor who wants to join," he said as he disappeared to probably get that visitor.

"*Mike*," I whined. I hated meeting guests whatsoever—especially if I wasn't mentally or physically prepared. "You know I hate surprise visits."

"Not this one you won't," his voice replied from the hallway. He came back with a purple cage I knew too well.

"Back *already*?" I jumped off the bed and gently grabbed it from him.

"Yeah, they said she needed to be with her owner for emotional support." His smile grew wider.

"Uh-oh. Why does she need emotional support?"

"Because a pregnant female can have pretty rough moods."

"Oh, my goodness, are you *serious*?" I squealed. I couldn't believe this.

"Who's pregnant?" Elora whipped her head around, eyes wide.

"Candy's expecting kittens in eight to nine weeks," Mike stated. "And according to her vet, being beside her owner is best for her.

"Aw, that's *so cute* I can't handle it,' Elora huddled beside me as I set the cat carrier on the floor and sat facing it.

"Hey, Candy," I cooed as I opened the door. "Did you miss me, girl?"

I heard her shift inside the carrier.

"She fell asleep on our way here," Mike explained as he

sat on the bed, he, too, wanting to see her.

I saw the edge of her cute little paws as she stretched and her little yellow eyes reflecting the light.

After inspecting us for a few seconds, she purred and settled herself on my lap.

"I missed you too, my little cutie pie." I stroked her white-and-gray fur, happy that Candy was finally with me again.

"Where'd you send her off to exactly?" Elora asked as she set aside the carrier. "A cat training place?"

"There was this two-week cat program at the veterinarian's clinic," I began. "Sort of like a getaway vacation, but for cats."

"They have these activities where they get to socialize with other cats and ability training, something like that," Michael continued. "But they called Mom this morning and told her that Candy was pregnant, so she told me to pick Candy up on my way home."

I picked her up and hugged her, inhaling the sweet smell of her fur. "I missed you, my li'l baby."

"Oh, stop it, you and your cat," Elora huffed as she took her from me. "You're being weird."

"Says the girl who feeds her parrot with her at the dinner table."

"I don't know what you're talking about." She hid her

smile as she took her turn with my baby.

"I'm glad I have a pet, you know?" I commented as I watched Lora scratch Candy behind the ears. "They're like tiny, furry best friends."

"That's easy for you to say," Mike huffed and glared.

"What?" I raised an eyebrow. "You and I both know a snake won't do in this household."

"Whoa," Elora joined in. "A snake? Seriously?"

"What? It seemed like a pretty good companion," he shrugged.

"I hate to break it to you," I stifled a giggle. "But you're not Voldemort."

"Ha ha." He rolled his eyes.

"The girl has a point," Elora laughed. "Besides, don't you have your own mice now?"

"They don't really count as pets like they do as lab rats." Mike got up and made his way to the door. "I'd better go change. I'll be in my lab if you need anything."

Which, if translated, meant, "I'll probably just stay this way until bedtime."

9 WHAT TO EXPECT

When Saturday came along, I had been up since eight and annoyed the heck out of Elora with texts until she came over. I found Dad still asleep and woke him up too. I made the entire household breakfast afterwards and refilled Candy's food bowl. I texted Riley to confirm our meet-up at the mall this Friday and said something in Young Geographers' WhatsApp group *(note to self: first meeting next Monday.)*

At nine forty-five, Mike was back from the pet store with mouse cheese. Lora, Candy, and I were in Mike's lab, and Dad was finishing up some work before joining us upstairs.

"Okay, guys, it's ten sharp," Mike began, his tone even more excited than last Tuesday. "The mice should be coming in from last week any minute now."

"*Mice?*" Elora asked as she slurped her strawberry milkshake from breakfast. "How many *did* you send?"

"Just five. Three on my own, once with you two, and once when all of us were there. Well, and once when, you know . . ." He shrugged as he looked at me. That wasn't a very . . . comfortable subject of discussion recently.

"How are you sure it'll work?" I couldn't help asking him. "I mean, *I'm sorry*, I still am, but the Time Explorer doesn't work anymore. How can you be sure the mice are coming?"

"Well, we did see cheese last week, didn't we?" He hesitated, then said, "The machine is programmed so that only the chair itself travels through time; not the entire machine. Or to its twin set somewhere in the past or future. The chair travels alone."

"Sounds cool, but what if—" Dad abruptly ceased talking as a small orb of blue lightning formed where the Time Explorer 3000 once stood (we had moved what was left of it farther into the attic).

The sphere began increasing in size, bigger and bigger, until the chair formed out of nothingness and the first mouse came into view.

Candy's eyes lit up and her head perked, but I kept a firm grip on her as I continued to stroke her behind the ears.

"You're filming this, right?" Michael asked, awestruck by what he was seeing.

"Uh-huh," Elora nodded, her eyes glued to the video-recording screen.

Mike hurried and took his notes and measurements and added a cube of cheese in the cage before the mouse was gone within a couple of minutes.

"That. Was. *Awesome!*" I squealed, making Candy jump. I was sitting cross-legged on the floor some distance away from the spot where the chair was earlier, my feline purring on my lap.

"Candy, you fat cat," I laughed and hugged her, once again happy that she was back. I never really noticed how much she meant to me until she left.

We resumed talking about things; school, the experiment, etc., before a few minutes later, the second mouse appeared. Then disappeared. After him the third, fourth, and fifth mice came along and disappeared, Mike as busy as a bumblebee throughout the process.

"This is really cool," Elora said as she aimed the camera at me. "What are your thoughts about this, Ms. Baker?"

"I think that my brother is an absolute genius!" I pretended to be talking into the "microphone" Elora was holding to my face. "By the way, how many mice are left?"

Mike turned to look at me, shrugged, and went back to his notes.

"Oh my God," I whispered. I was gonna see myself

again. Never thought it was a twice-in-a-lifetime experience.

We waited in silence for a few minutes before the now-familiar blue sphere popped up once more, bringing along with it an older version of me.

I got up and set Candy on Mike's desk, disbelieving my eyes. I looked at the scar-less Meghan, so innocently sitting in that chair; clueless of what was to come.

And I heard what I knew I was going to hear:

"How much did I get on my vocabulary test?"

"Eight out of ten," I immediately replied, even more freaked out than I was last week.

"Guys, the chair goes back in less than twenty seconds. So, uh, you might wanna step back," past Meg told us; we jumped back—*way back*.

The blue lightning encircled the chair once more as it started spinning; taking past Meg back where she came from.

"When the accident happens; nobody touch anything," Mike instructed.

We all stood back and I gathered Candy in my arms once more. Sure enough, the flickers of past me came and went. It was a horrifying view. We just waited until the flickering stopped and Meghan was back on Tuesday.

Michael began furiously writing down notes and the rest of us watched with awe.

"That was creepy," Elora commented as she stopped recording. "I mean, I'm glad you're okay, it's just that this, it looked creepy. But not that *you're* creepy, I—"

"It's fine," I shrugged, my eyes empty. That was the moment I got my scar. That was the moment I began having those creepy hallucinations. That's when trouble began.

"I'm heading downstairs." Dad broke my train of thoughts. "Your mom will kill me if we're late for her dentist appointment. And Mike," he went up to my brother and hugged him. "I'm *very* proud of you."

"Thanks, Dad." He hugged him back. I knew those words were what he yearned for since forever. His smile was satisfaction enough for me.

"I'm gonna go fix my thumb nail," Elora said as she headed for the stairs. "You coming?"

"In a sec . . ."

"I'll be in your room," her voice floated up the stairs.

"What is it, sis?" He sat down next to me and put his arm around me.

"Nothing," I shrugged. I was planning on telling him about my overly accurate déjà vu and scar, but something stopped me.

"You know you can talk to me, right?" he assured me.

I sighed. The scene changed. It was rainy outside and I was sitting on the floor, crying onto Mike's shoulder.

89

"It's okay." He hugged me tightly and rubbed my arm. "It's all right. Let it all out."

"It's j-just that I-I m-m-miss her *s-so much*," I managed to say between sobs.

"We all do," he comforted me, his voice sad too.

I pulled away and wiped my eyes. "I wish she didn't have to go." My voice was still shaking.

"We'll get through this. Together," he assured me once more.

And in a split second, the sky was morning once more and Mike was concernedly stroking my hair.

"You don't have to talk now," Mike was saying. "But I want to know when you feel comfortable sharing it. Is that okay?"

"Of course." I hugged him and stood up. "I trust you with everything."

I walked down the stairs, Candy tagging behind. She went straight for the food bowl in the kitchen as I went for my bedroom.

"Candy, you fat cat!" I laughed as I sat myself down on my bed.

"Why'd you call her fat?" Elora asked from my desk, busy with repainting her nails. "That's mean."

"Her appetite has almost doubled since she came

back," I explained as I lay down and stared up at the ceiling. "Poor pregnant little kitty needs to eat a lot now."

"It's only natural," Elora replied in her philosophical tone. "She needs to eat for her and the babies." She paused for a bit then asked, "How many weeks in is she?"

"Almost two," I absentmindedly replied. My mind was swimming with what I just saw. Why was I crying? And why did these vision-things happen to me? I knew they were too powerful to be just normal hallucinations.

That night I called Riley.

"Hey, Riles!" I chirped once she picked up.

"Hey, Meg! How's Sour Face?" she replied from the other end of the line.

"Still sour," I laughed. I told her almost everything. I enjoyed catching her up on what was going on with me, and in turn listening to her adventures and mischievous shenanigans.

"Hey, listen," I began, cutting to the point. "You're in medical college, right?"

"Sure am! Why? Is there anything wrong?"

"Well, I've been having these weird . . . hallucinations recently. I don't know, like illusions, déjà vu or something, and they're really strong. Is there, like, anything wrong with me?"

She hesitated.

"How often do you get these . . . illusions?" she finally asked after pondering what I said for a while.

"At random times of day. And they're about everything. You know, from things in class to stuff at home."

"Well, if you're *certain* they're hallucinations, there *is* a case, but from certain chemicals only."

"What? No!" I was shocked. "I would never!"

"I know, which is why it's eerie—" She stayed silent for a while, then said, "Sleep deprivation is dangerous to health as well. You're probably just worn out. Try to get some more sleep and tell me if you get better, all right? You can start now."

"Sure, I'll try. Goodnight!"

"G'night."

That call was as useful as a white crayon on white paper. I sighed as I sat down on my bed. This was getting out of hand. I had to tell Mike.

I heard the tiny paw steps up the stairs and looked at my doorway, waiting for the moment Candy stuck half her head in, then came "jogging" towards me.

I lifted her up and hugged her. She began purring instantly. Ever since she came back, she'd had an increased need for affection and attention from me.

It gave me a little happiness that she became closer to me and, well, kind of avoided the rest of my family. Hey, I felt special, don't judge.

I saw her face change and that's when I knew it was coming. I cradled her in my arms and quickly went downstairs and onto our front lawn.

I scrunched up my nose as she vomited onto the dirt near the sidewalk and went to drink from the water pipes. At least she cleaned herself.

I led her inside and sat down on the living room couch, pondering everything. A silver-blue scar. Weird illusions. A pregnant cat. What else was gonna come?

Candy went and ate a bit more. *Fat kitty*, I thought, but couldn't help smiling. Candy was the best thing that had happened to me.

I was gonna be a mom to even more cats! As she hopped up on my lap, I stroked her fur. I thought of the first day I got her.

I had been begging Mom and Dad for three months to get me a cat. I was overjoyed when they finally got me my dear little British shorthair.

I put her first—all the time. I watched her grow and cared for her for three years. She was really special to me.

I looked into her tired eyes and smiled as I continued to rub her below the chin. I loved the soft purr vibration on my lap.

I showered her with kisses one last time and put her

beside me and got up; her following suit.

As soon as I headed for the stairs, she dashed ahead of me and was in her little bed when I walked into my bedroom.

I put on my pajamas and wiggled my toes under the cold bedcovers. I couldn't get those . . . visions out of my head. Eventually, I promised myself to tell everything to Mike tomorrow; and the sooner the better.

I had a feeling I was going to procrastinate getting *that* done, too.

10 THE DEVIL WEARS PUMPS

By the following week, the scar news had died down.

Because someone had a *better* offer.

"Did you hear about Sarah?" Talia asked me right after assembly.

"I *literally* just got here. No, I haven't."

"She claims that her dad got her *Grammy tickets*." Penny joined our little huddle. "Can you *believe* that?"

"That's *so* cool," I gasped. *Grammy tickets?* Her dad must be *really* important.

"It seems highly unlikely." Elora rolled her eyes. "Sarah would do *anything* to have attention on herself."

"I know, but it seems real." Olivia appeared at our side. "She even told us *Shawn Mendes* personally called her to confirm a limo for pickup at the airport and escort her to the awards."

"Are you really buying all of this?" Elora laughed. "I cannot believe you're actually buying this." She shook her head in disbelief. "If Shawn Mendes did call her, then I'm not Elora Black."

"Lora, it *is* possible to get Grammy tickets, just hard," Talia argued.

"Where's your proof?"

Everyone fell silent.

"I'm not buying it until there's proof." Elora crossed her arms.

"She has a point, you know." I hid my giggles as I watched their struck faces. Elora was a girl who always had it her way; I thought everybody knew that by now.

"Meghan!"

I cringed. That high-pitched, irritating voice was another one of the reasons my head was gonna explode soon.

"Hey, Sarah." I turned to face her and wore the best fake smile I ever did in my life.

"So, Dad got us Grammy tickets," she began in her *I'm-going-to-make-you-so-jealous* tone. "And I was thinking if maybe you'd like to tag along! You know, since you're such a nice friend and all."

"And that, you know, your scar doesn't seem to be working anymore. Since you're not 'the talk,' you could use a little popularity boost."

She gave me a side-look and glared, her two cronies (Nicole from nine-3 and Kandice from our class) snickering.

Calling me her tag-along was one thing; making fun of me like that was another.

"Oh, Sarah," I laughed and waved my hand dismissively. "It's not like every day you get a Grammy ticket. But unless your name is Google, don't act like you know everything and everyone." I was furious. "So, thanks but no thanks; I'll pass on the offer. Oh, and tell Queen Bey I say hi!"

She gritted her teeth and her face was so twisted I could've sworn it was partially permanently deformed. I could see her mutter something under her breath before huffing and walking away.

"Sheesh, who knew a new student could be so snobbish?" Talia shook her head as she watched Sarah high-heel away.

"Meghan, Meghan, *Meghan*." Elora shook her head as she looked at me disapprovingly. "When did you become so shady?" And high-fived me.

"We need two ice-cold water buckets for that burn," Penny laughed as she high-fived me as well.

"Yeah, but don't you think that was a bit . . . mean?" Olivia interrupted.

Talia, Elora, and Penny swiveled towards her.

"No, it *wasn't!* She simply stood up for all the girls Sarah was mean to before," Talia argued.

"That comeback wasn't mean; it just put her in her place," Penny added.

"It was just a thought." Olivia rolled her eyes and laughed. "No need to argue."

"Did you see her though? You definitely did get to her," Elora sniggered. "Watch out, Meg, she's got it in for you now."

"Oooh, I'd better sleep with one eye open." I faked shivering.

"Girls, didn't you hear the bell?" Mrs. McAllister, our math teacher, frowned at us from the other side of the lawn. "Your class has begun!"

We apologized in unison and followed her to nine-2, suppressing our giggles.

***

The first two lessons dragged by, every second multiplying into a minute, every minute into an hour. It took *ages* to finally finish the ninety minutes of mathematical torture.

When the bell signaling the end of math and the beginning of English finally rang, Ms. Avery was already at the door.

"Good morning," she smiled to Mrs. McAllister as she left the class, who replied with an arched eyebrow and left.

"Girls, please pass your assignments to the first bench," she instructed us as she took care of the boards. "I will be collecting them in a couple of minutes."

"Give me your assignment," Elora told me, the papers of all the girls behind us in her hand.

"I didn't do it," I replied, my face a combination of worry and uneasiness.

Elora's jaw dropped. "*What?* Ms. Avery's going to *kill* you!"

"I'll figure something out." I brushed it off, feeling a bit queasy. *Or at least I hope I do.*

After Mrs. Avery collected our assignments, Sarah's hand shot up in the air.

"Yes, Sarah?"

"Ms. Avery, I just wanted to notify you that you didn't collect Meghan's paper." Her strong voice went over the noise of the class. That disgusting smirk on her face said everything I needed to know.

"Why? Didn't you pass it to the front, Meghan?" She turned to me.

"Erm, no," I admitted. "I didn't do it yet."

"Meghan, that's one time too many." She looked at me with a raised eyebrow. She didn't raise her voice. She didn't make any angry faces. She just spoke in that monotone that sent shivers down my body. "You can turn it in with last week's missed book report; I expect it on my desk by Thursday."

"I won't let you down," I smiled weakly.

As if Sarah wasn't angry enough, Ms. Avery turned towards her.

"And, Sarah? Nobody likes a snitch."

You could hear the ripple of snickers across the class. Elora was overjoyed.

"*Ha*! That'll teach her to tell on other students." She smirked Sarah's way.

"Or be mean to anyone," Talia added, turning around in her seat. "I think Sarah's about to see what being the class diva will bring for her." She fist-bumped Elora.

As Ms. Avery began revising active and passive voice with the class, another one of my illusion thingies came into focus.

We were in our class—geography, by the looks of it—and Mrs. Kartley was standing by Olivia's desk.

Principal Shirley was standing facing us, her old wrinkles absorbing her overdone makeup. She pointed her long, manicured nail at Sarah and motioned for her to come forward.

"Uh, me?" Sarah pointed at herself, looking startled.

"Yes."

She got up and walked to the front of the class, her heeled boots breaking the pin-drop silence.

The principal set a firm hand on her shoulder and began in her hawk-like voice, 'This is the best example"—Sarah's face lit up for a split second—"of a student in bad attire. This is not how you dress in school."

Sarah winced as the principal's grip tightened.

"Full-face makeup, above-knee dress, and *heels*."

She turned Sarah to stand facing her.

"Detention, young lady. For coming to an education facility dressed like a dancer. I will not tolerate these kinds of actions in school."

And with that, she walked out of the class and I was snapped back to English. Except Mrs. Avery was staring at me.

"Meghan, are you okay?" Her face looked at me with concern.

"What?" I looked around. The entire class was staring. "*Oh*, yeah . . . I'm fine." I shook my head to get rid of the spinning sensation I got.

"Are you *sure*?"

"Yeah, yeah. I'm good."

"Do you know the answer to the question?"

"Uh . . ." I mentally kicked myself. I was always put in this kind of situation whenever my stupid hallucinations kicked in. "What was the question again?"

"What's the definition of the active voice?" Her eyes looked at me with unsettlement.

"The active voice is, uh . . . a sentence where the *subject* does the action, I think?" My mind was empty. I tried digging in to find anything I could say. "The order of the sentence is usually subject, then the verb, then the object."

"Very good." It took a while for her to look away from me. "Alex, can you give me an example?"

As the class debated on sentences, my thoughts were all over the place. *What was that?*

I got more worried with every passing minute, anxious to go home and tell everything to Michael.

I hoped with all my heart that they'd leave me alone for the rest of the day—my horrible illusions, or whatever they were. I was so fidgety throughout the entire day that no useless spinner would be able to fix me.

I sighed heavily as the bell marking the end of the day rang. I hadn't had any more delusional visions since the English incident.

Elora helped me pack up, and we didn't even stay a second longer to hang out after school. As we headed for the entrance Elora looked at me, a worried expression in her eyes. I raised my eyebrow in question, but she just shrugged and looked at the road ahead of us.

Once we were out of earshot though, she began. "Hey, I've been meaning to talk to you . . . what's up with you these days?"

"What do you mean?" I tried to hide my lying face as I warmed my hands inside my hoodie's pocket.

"You know what I mean." She poked me as we walked over some dead leaves. "You've been spacing out a lot lately. For no apparent reason."

"I don't know what you're talking about," I simply replied.

"*Meghan*," she whined. "Come on! Tell me!"

"What's there to say?"

"Why are you so absentminded lately? What are you always thinking about? Why do you seem to be on cloud nine all the time?" She hesitated for a moment. "We're *best friends*. You're supposed to trust me!"

"I do trust you!"

"Then *tell me*."

I sighed heavily as we walked on in silence. "I . . ."

I didn't know what to say.

"If you don't tell me, our friendship is *over*," she said, breaking the silence.

"*What*?! Lora, it's no big deal."

"If it isn't, then tell me!" She paused before saying, "Tell me or I won't *ever* forgive you."

"Lora, *please*." I looked at her pleadingly. She just turned her nose away from me and walked on.

"*Fine*." I gave in. "Just . . . I'll tell you once we get home, okay?"

"Deal." She smiled satisfactorily and skipped ahead of me. I felt a knot form in the pit of my stomach. *This is bad.*

11 WEIGHT OFF MY SHOULDERS

When we got home, Elora wouldn't stop nagging me about what was wrong.

"Just *tell* me!" she badgered, over and over.

"Okay, okay," I said at last. "Just . . . let me go change?"

"*One. Last. Chance.*" She narrowed her eyes as I made my way upstairs.

I took my phone out as soon as I made it to my bedroom and dialed Riley's number.

"Hey! It's Riley here. I'm a bit busy right now, so leave a voicemail and I'll get back to you when I can!"

I sighed as the voicemail beep played.

"Uh, hey, Riles! Listen, I uh, need to talk to you as soon as possible. Call me when you can. It's um . . . about my illusions. Thanks."

I pressed the end button and sat on my bed.

"*What were you doing?*"

The sudden voice startled me. I turned around to see Elora in the doorway, fury in her eyes.

"I was just . . ." I stammered. *Busted.*

"Were you calling *Riley?*"

"No! Well, yes, but—"

"What illusions were you talking to her about?"

"Well, you see—"

"Have you told her something *I don't know?*"

"Elora, I trust you with my life. I know I can tell you everything—"

"Except you didn't." She stood cross-armed in the doorway.

"I was going to—"

"You've been avoiding telling me this since—since *forever!*"

"Elora, some things are private."

"How come you told Riley?"

"She's a doctor."

"A *doctor? Seriously?* She's *still studying!*"

"She's qualified enough to know what she's saying."

"Oh, so you're defending her now?"

"I'm stopping *you* from maintaining false ideas about her."

"Ugh, me? *Me?* Meghan, I know very well that you've told Riley a million things that you didn't even consider talking about with me."

"Seriously? Like what? Riley is just my cousin who I just so happen to trust."

"*Just so happen?* Please, you tell her *everything.*"

"Give me an example."

"Hm, lemme think . . . Riley picked your outfits. Riley knows about your fears. Riley helps you with your problems. Riley is who you call when you need advice. And now, Riley knows what's been bothering you for the past week and not once have I crossed your mind!"

"You didn't think I was here to talk? You didn't think I would've been willing to sneak out of my house to help? You didn't think that I, your *real* best friend, am trustworthy? I don't even know half the things you told her! And now you refuse to tell me what on earth is going on with you!"

"Elora, you're being ridiculous. You *are* my best friend."

"Yeah, that's obvious. Especially since you go and tell *Riley* everything."

"Lora, stop it. You're just jealous."

"*Jealous*? Oh, so now my concern about you is jealousy."

I could see beads of tears in her eyes as she struggled to keep them in.

"Elora, there are some things that I feel I should ask a grown-up about; for an older opinion."

"That's not what I—you're missing the *entire point*." She sighed and shook her head. "If you don't see me as necessary, then I guess we just shouldn't be friends anymore."

"*That's* your solution? Ending everything? Just because I haven't told you a few things?"

"You see them as a few things, huh? Proves further that you obviously don't need this friendship."

"*Fine*!"

"*FINE*!"

And with that, she stormed out of the room. I heard her angry footsteps barrel down the stairs and saw her leave the house from my window.

I threw myself onto my bed as I felt my eyes begin to water up, too. Didn't she *understand*? She's mad at me for being tired and confused and trapped inside my own mind— *every single day!* This is hard for me! I must live with myself every day with stupid, delusional scenes in my head.

And now she'd left me. Just like that. It wasn't my fault. *None of this* is my fault. My head began throbbing in pain as I closed my eyes and felt the tears roll down onto my bed.

"Everything okay?"

I got up to see Michael standing in the doorway, a concerned look on his face.

"Does it *look* like I'm okay? Of course not!"

I instantly felt bad for lashing out at him like that.

"Sorry, I just . . ." I wiped the tears from my eyes with the back of my sleeve. I shook my head as he sat down beside me. "I don't know."

"Well, follow me." He pulled me up and dragged me behind him.

"Where are we going?"

"Somewhere we can talk." He slid open my window and imitated my moves from last time; gracefully climbing to where we'd sat just last week.

"Come on up." He patted the space next to him.

I sighed and followed him up.

"Do you wanna talk about what just happened?"

"No," I replied, a little bit too aggressively. "It's just that Elora can be very *stubborn* at times."

"Okay." He looked at me and smiled. "Then we're

gonna talk about what *I* want to know."

"What is it?"

"Oh, gallant warrior, do present to me your scar." He waved his hand royally and smirked. "Come on, show me."

I felt shock run through me. *How did he find out?* Nevertheless, I couldn't help smiling at his lame presentation.

"Come on, Maha told me everything," he urged.

"Okay, but don't feel bad."

"I *promise*, I'm over that. You're in decent shape. I just need to see it to analyze what my baby can do!"

I gave him the evilest smile I could muster. "Do you think you're ready?"

"Just show me!"

I pulled up my left sleeve and flashed him my silver-blue beauty. "How's *that* for cool measure?"

"Oh, my God," he whispered. "This is incredible! I need a sample and details when we get down, deal?"

"You got yourself a deal, Dr. Michaelstein," I said as I pulled my sleeve back down and firmly shook his hand.

"Wow, that scar is like *nothing* the world has seen!" He shook his head in disbelief. "Fantastic."

Then my mind flashed back to last time we were on the

roof. When I had this . . . *powerful vision describing exactly what happened just now.*

"Yeah, I-I have some things I want to talk to you about too," I confessed. "It's been bothering me for a week now and I have nobody else to talk to."

"I assumed you would've told Elora."

I cringed at the mention of her name. "Let's *not* bring her up for now. Although I did tell Riley."

"Sorry. So, tell me!"

"Okay, so I've been getting these kinds of visions that are weird. At first, I thought they were hallucinations, but I realize they are too strong to be. I've been thinking they might be tricks my mind is playing on me, but I don't know."

His forehead was creased with concentration. "What kind of visions?"

"Like, I'd be me, but at another time doing other things. Take now, for example. I saw myself last week showing you the scar, then the exact same thing happened now. Or when I saw that Mrs. Evans was passing out test papers, and the next day she actually gave us a pop quiz. Stuff like that. It comes at random times and for I don't know how long. And when I have them, it's like I'm not here anymore. I just have no idea what happens here."

He nodded his head, lost in thought. "You say you see

things and then they happen?"

"Basically."

I took a deep breath of fresh air and smiled. Finally. A huge weight off my shoulders. I had someone to go to whenever these pesky visions ruined my day.

"Meghan." Mike finally turned to me, a huge smile on his face. "I have a theory."

"Propose your idea, Mr. Baker."

"I think you can see the future."

12 I SEE YOU

A few minutes later, I was in Michael's lab, in a chair, with a bunch of monitors around me.

"All we need to prove my theory correct is for you to have a foreshadow, and these machines here will record everything," he explained.

"Don't I have to wear a scientific detection helmet thing?" I asked, unsure of what to expect.

"I'm glad you mentioned that." He made me wear the metal headgear and stood back.

"Now go." He motioned for me to begin. Not sure to begin what though.

"What am I supposed to do?" I asked.

"Just have a foreshadow."

"How?"

He thought in silence for a minute. "Think of the future. What was one thing you had in common when you got your visions?"

"I'd be worried or excited or anxious . . ."

"About?"

"About what was going to happen," I realized as the words left my mouth. I just needed to think that I wanna know what will happen.

I closed my eyes, my heart racing. What was I supposed to think about? Me? School? *Elora?* I shook her out of my head and thought of every other imaginable subject in my life.

I must've stayed that way for a long time, because I heard Michael suddenly talk.

"Okay, turns out it isn't manual," he sighed as he set his clipboard back down.

I took off my helmet and got off the seat.

"Sorry," I apologized as I stood next to him. "I tried the best I could."

"I know," he sighed. "Show me your scar."

He brought a small petri dish and a surgical knife.

"*What*?! You said you were gonna take a sample!" I pulled my uncovered arm away in panic.

"Calm down! You won't feel a thing!"

I hesitated. He was my own brother. He wouldn't hurt me. But the knife looked so intimidating . . .

"Fine." I gave him my trembling arm and he held it in place.

"Calm down," he assured me. "You're going to be fine."

I took deep breaths and settled myself. "Okay. Go ahead."

I felt a tiny prick when the knife scraped up a bit of skin. He set it on the dish and went over to his workbench.

I looked at my arm. *No blood.* Amazing.

"It's a bruise, by the way," he told me as he worked on his sample.

"What?"

"It's a bruise. Not a scar."

"Oh. Thanks for clarifying."

Why did all of this happen at once? First the scar—I mean, *bruise.* Then the visions. Followed by a mean school diva and a fight with Elora. Could things get any worse?

"I need a blue hydrangea," he suddenly piped up.

"What for?"

"The skin is perfectly normal; all layers as normal as they can get. The color is the only thing that has changed. I want to compare the pigment of this sample and a flower. According to my notes, it should be the same."

"Seriously? My skin is related to a plant?"

"Let the scientist do his work." He rolled his eyes as he set down his working glasses and got up. "You share fifty percent of your DNA sequence with a banana anyway. Let's go."

I followed him to our garden. The one *I* weeded last time. I hadn't forgotten to rub that in every time Mike came outside.

"Okay, okay, we get it." He began carefully examining Mom's hydrangeas while I sat below the tiny maple shared between us and our neighbors' backyards.

I was looking out at our other neighbors' lawn when the sky changed. The sky was sharing my mourning. Flowers were tossed out in front of me and Maha was beside me.

"She's in a better place now," she managed to say, tears streaming down her cheeks as well. "You should be happy."

"I didn't want her to go so soon." I set yet another flower amongst the others. "She went so young."

"I know." Maha closed her eyes. "We all miss her so much."

I closed my eyes too, but when I opened them, I was once again with Michael.

He had stopped picking flowers and was looking at me,

his face awed.

"You just had a foreshadow."

"Yeah," I half-told myself, half-told him.

"You had a glazed look," he continued, his eyes growing wider and his tone growing excited with every word. "Of course! The accident had a permanent effect on you!"

"Like the bruise?"

"Yes! Except the bruise was physical. It captured the color of the object it's in contact with. But your foreshadows, they're a mental effect. It recognized the incident and now your subconscious travels to your future self and back here!"

"What? Slow down, I'm lost."

"Your brain is the only thing that travels, not your entire body. Brilliant! Come on."

He grabbed my wrist and hoisted me up, then sprinted upstairs.

"Wait for me!" I struggled to keep up. When I reached the attic, he was already writing down a ton of things and looking through his folders.

"Yes, yes, yes! It all makes sense! Your mind travels forward in time, alone. It snaps back when someone awakens you, or grabs your attention!"

It all made sense now. Kind of. *Not really.*

"Meghan." He looked at me with a serious face. "Don't tell anyone."

"Even Mom and Dad?"

"Especially Mom and Dad." He walked up to me and stood facing me, his nose inches from mine. "If anyone finds out, they'll run experiments on you, and do God knows what to your subconscious. Mom and Dad would get worried and take you to a doctor, leading to exactly that. So be careful; don't mention this to *anyone*, and I mean *anyone*."

"Okay." The seriousness in his tone intimidated me. "Even if I told anyone, they wouldn't believe me."

"Then you'd be called crazy, mad, deranged, lunatic," he continued. "That's what normal people would do. But science fanatics, such as yours truly, would take it into consideration. They'd run tests on you to find out what's going on with you. That's bad."

And that's when fear really did kick in. *I can see the future?* What? I began feeling terror in my body. I had an insight on what was going to happen. Which endangered me to crazed scientists everywhere. *Everywhere.*

"Mike, you won't run tests on me, will you?" I couldn't help asking in a small voice.

"Of course not." He hugged me. "Nothing that could harm you. I've learned my lesson."

I looked back at him and smiled. "I mean, you *could* run just a few *minor* trials."

"Nothing dangerous," he assured me, smiling too.

"Thank you for not thinking I'm crazy." I hugged him.

"You already are crazy, you couldn't get any more than that."

"Hey!"

"I'm just kidding, you know."

"Yeah, right."

"But I'm serious. I do believe you."

"Thanks."

"What did you see in the garden, anyway?" he asked as he pulled away, looking at me with a questioning face.

I thought for a while. "Maha and I were somewhere, mourning over someone."

"Could you tell where that place was?"

"Not really." I squeezed my brain to remember. "All I remember is that there were flowers on the ground in front of us, it was raining, and Maha was comforting me."

He fell silent for a while. "Listen, this new power you have is a gift and a burden. Don't let these foreshadows control your present. It's just a few seconds from the future. You don't know for sure what it means. Don't let these foreshadows change your way of seeing things or affect your decisions. Just pretend they don't even happen, okay?"

"Sure." I pondered what he said for a while. He made sense. "I won't let them control my actions."

"Good," he smiled, ruffling my hair, and went back to his flowers set on his workbench. "Are you going to help me or not?"

***

The rest of the day went by as great as ever. Mom (thankfully) never found out about the fight between me and Elora, because I know she would've interfered to fix things. Which would only make things worse.

I spent my time occasionally helping around the house and doing my homework—with Candy repeatedly sitting on my textbooks. I re-read our biology assignment and looked at it in confusion.

"Hey, Lora, what are we supposed to do for bio?" I asked my empty room. I swiveled in my chair and looked at my empty bed, where my best friend was supposed to be sitting. I felt bad as I resumed my work, distracted by everything that'd been happening . . . mostly Elora.

"How would you feel if I slept over in your room this evening?" Maha asked me before bedtime, her face filled with hope.

"Well," I weighed the options. There was no reason I

could say no, but I didn't want to say yes, either.

"I promise I won't kick you in my sleep," she assured me.

I sighed heavily and hesitated. "Sure, but on one condition."

"Anything!"

"You bring your own pillow and blanket."

"Done!" She dashed to her room and left me laughing.

Moments later, we were both in our pajamas and settled under our blankets, side by side on my bedroom floor.

"Goodnight, Meg." She yawned as she turned to face me.

"Goodnight," I replied as her eyes drooped and closed.

But I couldn't sleep. I kept tossing and turning, contemplating my recent "foreshadows." First the near car crash. Then the denial. Lastly came the mourning and crying. My heart raced in my ribs as I tried to think of something, *anything* else, with no use. My mind was whirring with unpleasant thoughts I didn't want to mention.

I had accidentally predicted an unavoidable future, and it was terrifying.

13 THE GIFT OF A (BEST) FRIEND

The next day, Maha was my chat partner on our way to school.

". . . I mean, you and Elora always hang out together," she continued. "When Kira's mom said I could go back home with her, I was beyond happy! You and Lora are absolute goals, honestly. Which is why I'm thrilled I get to leave with Kira every day, you know?"

"Yeah." I bit my lip in guilt. "I'm so happy for you."

I felt horrible. We'd fought over something *so silly*. I had to talk to her, and the sooner, the better.

"Meg, is it okay if we do this more often?" Maha asked me when the school came into view.

"Do what more often?" I asked.

"You know, walk to school together. You always talk

with Elora on our way to school. I had fun talking with you this morning." She stopped and looked at me hopefully. "If it's okay, I mean."

"Of course!" I replied enthusiastically. "I had fun too." *And it's gonna happen more often soon, whether I choose to or not.*

I shook my head firmly to rid myself of that thought. No. It was *not* gonna happen. Elora will *still* be my partner on our way to school until we graduate . . .

If my foreshadows were wrong.

When I walked into class, Elora wasn't sitting in her usual seat. Instead, she sat in Alex's place, since she was absent.

"Why is Elora sitting over there?" Olivia asked me when I took my seat.

"Probably to hang out with Leah," I replied. I felt it better to not mention that we were not on speaking terms.

I waited for the chance, any chance at all, to talk to her, but it was as if the teachers were plotting against me. Every lesson went without a hitch, us working nonstop like bumblebees. One lesson finished, the other one began.

It wasn't until lunchtime that I got the chance, and once the bell rang, she was out of class with Leah and Penny.

By the time I left our classroom, they had already disappeared. I was looking in the hallways when I heard her voice from outside.

"Why would you even *do* that?" I heard Elora argue.

"Elora, please," I heard Sarah reply. "Don't interfere in what's not your business."

"Funny you should say that, since *you* do that all the time," Elora shot back, obviously irritated.

"Really? Was that supposed to be a burn? Because I felt nothing."

I was *not* gonna let her be rude to my best friend like that.

"Yeah, that's because you're already roasted." I appeared at Elora's side. Our argument could wait. I heard several girls gasp at my retort and laugh under their breath.

"Nobody asked for your opinion," Sarah replied agitatedly, and narrowed her eyes at me.

"Neither for yours," I replied simply.

"You should do as I told your 'friend' here and stay out of what doesn't concern you." She flashed her annoying fake smile at me.

"I'm pretty sure what concerns my *best* friend concerns me, too," I retorted.

Her face was beginning to transform into red. Perfect.

"By the way, where's your off button? I think we all need a break here." Elora smirked.

"How *dare* you?" she screeched, and turned her back on us and left.

"Good one." She high-fived me, then her face returned to its expressionless state when she realized what she just did.

"Thank you!" Jennifer hugged Elora. "I wanted to talk back, but then I froze, I don't know why. And then she went on and talked about how I was lame, and I just got kind of . . . lost."

Jennifer was the youngest in our class; younger by a year and a half, no big deal. She was actually really nice, just a little bit of a . . . pushover. I suppose Sarah was teasing her about some fandom of hers or her "awfully young age."

"There are six people I despise on this earth and three of them are Sarah," Elora replied with a smirk.

"I'd say the same, but she might hold an even *bigger* grudge on me," Jennifer laughed, and waved before walking away.

"Hey, listen," I began. "We need to talk, about yesterday."

Elora raised an eyebrow. "Go ahead."

"Okay . . . *I'm sorry.*" I forced the heavy words out like a burden. I *hated* apologizing, not to mention bluntly saying *sorry*. I felt a lot better after saying it though, and the relieved look on Lora's face made me feel okay.

She sighed heavily and smiled back. A small one, but still a smile. "I'm sorry too." She looked anywhere but at me. "I guess I was maybe a little . . . fiercely protective of one's rights or possessions."

The last words left her lips at such a bare whisper I almost missed it.

"What?" I looked at her in confusion.

"You heard me," she shrugged. "Look it up."

So, I did. I inconspicuously reached for my phone in my hoodie's pocket and quickly typed it in. The google page with the results popped up; *jealous* / ˈdʒɛləs/ - *fiercely protective of one's rights or possessions.*

"A*www*," I smiled a little, feeling warm inside. She was *jealous.* Is it weird that I was happy? For me, it meant that she cared enough about me to want me to be *her* best friend only.

"I know I shouldn't be . . ." her voice trailed off.

"Trust me, Riley is nowhere near our level of closeness. Did I ever come to her house spontaneously in the middle of the night because she was crying?"

"How am I supposed to know? You might've done it without me seeing you." She shrugged as I rolled my eyes at her.

"Well, the answer is no, I never did, and never will. Trust me, *you're* my better half. Nobody knows me like you

126

do. Besides, you can't replace what's irreplaceable, right?"

"*Awww*, you flatter me." She fanned her face as I laughed, hiding my phone safely back in my pocket. I caught my breath before pulling her into a hug. A warm, comforting hug only a best friend can give.

"I know I should've told you, it's just that I was just . . . nervous, confused, I dunno," I spoke up. "Next time, I promise I'll tell *you* everything. Forgive me?"

She pulled back and nodded her head, a wide grin etched on her face. "Thanks. Now come on; Liv and the rest are probably wondering where we've been."

She linked her arm through mine as we made our way to our usual spot. I was just grateful we were on speaking terms again, the uneasy thoughts creeping into my brain every now and then. *Why do I have to have foreshadows?*

***

I unlocked the front door, letting Elora in before me as I safely put my keys back in my backpack.

"Let's not be on not-speaking terms again, okay?" she commented. "I had *so much* to tell you last night. And for God's sake, don't hide anything from me; you can trust me with anything."

"Okay and okay," I laughed as she flung her bag onto the nearest chair.

Then I remembered our argument in the first place—

my foreshadows. How could I *not* tell Elora? The words were like a jack-in-the-box, impatient and ready to jump out at any minute. But I kept my promise to Mike and bit my tongue, forcing my lips to not mention any of it.

"Anything to snack on?" she asked, already headed for the kitchen.

I nodded distractedly. *Where is Michael?*

As I took off my jacket and boots, I heard the rumble of Michael's car outside. I opened the door just as he was fumbling with his keys.

"Did your psychic powers tell you I was coming?" he joked as he too stepped in and took off his jacket.

"Yeah, that's what I wanted to talk to you about," I confessed.

"What? Did anything change about them?"

"No, they're the same." I struggled to find the words. "But I think there's a certain someone who *deserves* to know."

"Elora?" He wore that knowing smile. "I thought you might say that. I was weighing the options for the past few hours, and I guess she's safe."

I squealed and clapped my hands in glee.

"But *only* Elora," he emphasized.

"Don't worry, I don't intend to tell anybody else." I hugged him and went to the kitchen.

"These mini cupcakes are wicked good," Elora commented when I walked in, the plate in her hands. "I'm even surprised there are leftovers." She popped an entire cupcake in her mouth.

"I'm glad you like them," I smiled. "Now come on, there's something really important I need to tell you."

"Okay, go ahead," she managed to say while chewing.

"No, in my room." I tilted my head towards the stairs.

"Why?"

"It's not safe here."

She narrowed her eyes at me for a while, then put the plate back in the fridge and followed me upstairs.

"Why don't you want anybody to hear?" she asked suspiciously as she plopped down on my bed.

"Because Mike thinks my parents are better off not knowing about it," I explained as I silently closed the door and took a seat on my spinning chair. "And my mom might show up any minute."

"Okay, you're making me nervous." Elora raised an eyebrow. "What's going on?"

"Promise not to tell a single soul. Not even your *family*."

"I promise. *Double* promise."

"Well . . ." I looked for the words. What *do* I say? *Oh hey, I can see the future, how cool is that?*

"I uh, kinda can see . . . the future?"

"What?"

"Mike calls them foreshadows. That glazed look I've been getting? Yeah, that's when my mind travels to the future for an unset amount of time."

"Wait." Elora looked at me, her face shocked. "You're telling me you can literally *see the future*? Like, a psychic?"

"Basically, yeah," I shrugged. That was a sentence I never expected to hear.

Elora stared at me for a moment, then doubled over with laughter. I just stared at her in disbelief.

"Good one, Meghan!" She shook her head when she managed to catch her breath. "You got me, though. I really thought something was up with you."

"Elora, I'm serious!"

"That was a really good prank!"

"It's not!" I looked at her seriously. How could she laugh? This was *horrible* for me. And her reaction was comedic. *Seriously*?

"Really? Lemme guess, you're on a show now. Oooh, I know! *That's So Meghan*!"

"What?"

"That's so Meghan, it's the future I can see," she began singing.

"Elora . . ."

"That's so Meghan, it's so mysterious to me!"

"Elora! I'm one hundred percent, certainly, perfectly serious! What I'm saying is true!"

She stopped singing and her smile faded away.

"Meg, cut the jokes."

"This is *no joke.*" I was hurt at how she took it in such a funny way. "This is actually happening to me."

I'm guessing the look on my face was solemn, because she stopped messing around and looked unsettled.

"Are you for real?" she asked in an undertone.

"That's what I've been trying to say!"

She stared unblinkingly at me for a while.

"That's so cool," she breathed.

"You mean, you're not freaked out? You don't think I'm crazy?"

"I am and I do. I just believe that you're saying the truth."

"Okay," I hesitantly smiled. "That's reassuring."

"So . . . can you predict something?" she awkwardly asked.

"It's not up to me," I shrugged. "It just happens."

"When was the last time you . . . uh . . . had a . . . foreshadow?"

"This morning, during chemistry."

"What did you see?"

"I saw myself holding one of Candy's kittens." I tried to remember. "She was blondish, and apparently I had named her Caramel."

"*Cute!*" she squealed. "What else?"

"I don't know, just trivial things. Like I'd see myself in an IT class, or taking a test, maybe at home helping Dad, stuff like that."

Or see you in a car crash.

"That's awesome." Elora's eyes were as wide as tennis balls. "You can actually see it?"

"I can live it."

We sat in silence for a moment or two.

Then I was facing my desk, tackling my math homework. There were three kittens playing with my pencil case; one blond, one black, and the third grey-and-white.

I was solving a particularly tough equation when the black one began playing with my pencil as I was writing.

"Oh, Oreo," I sighed as I patted her tiny back. "You miss her too, don't you?"

She gave me a tiny meow in response.

"Yeah, I miss her presence too."

I fell silent for a few moments.

"I just can't help but think . . . how different it would've been if she was still around. If I could still see her every day."

I spun my chair around, staring at the ceiling, thinking of whoever *she* was. When I stopped, Elora was back on the bed, staring at me open-mouthed.

"You just had a foreshadow," she gasped.

"Yeah . . ." I slowly nodded.

"What did you see?"

"I was doing my math homework with three kittens on my desk." I decided to leave out the conversation I had.

"Oooh, what were their colors? And their names?"

"One was blond, the other grey-and-white, and the third black. The blond, I'm guessing, was Caramel. I know the black one was Oreo."

"Aw, they sound adorable." She imagined the baby kittens. "I can't wait to meet them."

I hope so.

Quit it, Meghan! I mentally scolded myself for letting my brain wander in that train of thought. *Elora's staying.*

We sat in silence for a few more moments before Elora piped up in a reassuring tone, "It'll be fine. I'll help you with the foreshadows."

"Thanks." My mouth transformed into a small smile.

"I'm serious! We'll go through it together. Even if someday you get a vision that's unsettling."

"You have *no idea.*"

14 FRENEMIES

You can call me paranoid, but I was overly anxious for the next few days. I made sure everything even slightly dangerous was out of Elora's way.

I considered telling Mike, but he'd give me that "don't let the future fool you" lecture. So, I was on my own.

Sometimes I told myself that I was stupid to try and change the future. That it was inevitable that she'd . . . leave, and I'd have to make the most of my time with her. But then a little spark of hope would push me to keep trying.

And this Thursday was no different. Mrs. Greene gave us her physics lesson so we could plan on our science fair projects.

Elora, Leah, Jessica, and I were drawn as a group.

"How about we make a cell structure?" Leah was the

first to suggest.

"Nah, too lame," Elora replied dismissively. "We need something that actually *works;* with moving parts and all."

"What if we made"—Jessica thought for a while—"oooh, rocket science! Baking soda plus vinegar equals . . . lift off!"

"Still too *basic,*" Elora mumbled, her brow furrowed in concentration. "Meghan? Do you have anything?"

"Nah," I shrugged. "You come up with the idea; I'll apply it."

"I've got it!" Leah snapped her fingers. "We program a machine to play a song on a piano!"

"Okay," Elora pondered. "But where's the wow factor in that? It's just simple programming to press the keys in order."

"I know!" Jessica jumped in. "We try the fire in a bottle experiment! You can't go wrong with fire, right?"

"Perfect!" Elora nodded. "We'll blow their heads off! Well, not literally, but just enough that we win first prize."

"I love it!" Leah added. "The danger in the experiment; it's the perfect thing to win us first place."

My head jerked up at the word "danger." *What? No way.*

"No!" I suddenly blurted. "I mean, we can't do *that.*"

"Why not?" Jessica raised her eyebrows. I hated when

she did that.

"Because . . . I don't think the school"—I squeezed my brain for a good enough excuse—"would allow us . . . to conduct such a *dangerous* experiment on campus."

"We'll convince the admins," Jessica argued. "We have pretty good persuasion—"

"*And* . . . I have a better idea for our project!" I interrupted.

"What could possibly be better than fire?" Leah challenged.

"A . . . volcano," I tried. "I mean, we know that volcanos *always* win. We can even add our own touch; like food coloring or a mountain view, stuff like that."

The three of them sat in silence for a few moments; sweat began forming on my forehead. It was a dumb idea, I know. I realized how stupid this was. How stupid *everything* was.

I wish I wasn't always distracted. I wish I never saw Elora in that foreshadow. I wish I never started having foreshadows. I wished I never agreed to help Mike with his experiment.

"You know, she has a point," Elora finally said. "Volcanos *do* always win. Ooh, and we could even add glitter! You know, so it explodes everywhere when the volcano erupts."

"If you're sure," Leah shrugged. "Sure, I'm in."

"Same here," Jessica added.

Thank God for Elora's leadership skills. I involuntarily exhaled deeply and began pitching in with what I thought would help our project win.

Until time changed.

Mrs. Kartley had just walked in with papers in her hands.

"Prepare yourselves, we have a pop quiz."

The entire class exploded in moaning and grumbling. Elora turned and looked at me in awe.

"My goodness, it's really *real*!"

"You didn't believe me?" I took the paper. The title read, *Quiz 6: The Arctic Ocean.*

"I'm sorry, I didn't *entirely* think it was true," Elora shook her head in disbelief. "But you're not a lunatic. You can see the future, all right."

I smiled satisfactorily and took my pen. *Ready to ace this test.*

"*Meg,*" Elora whispered urgently.

I looked at her, startled.

"You had a *foreshadow*?" she whispered to me as Leah and Jessica were fighting over something or other.

I nodded. "It was a darn good one, too."

"What was it?"

"Let's just say, we need to revise last week's geography lesson."

***

As I handed in my test with confidence (and a bit of relief), Elora turned to look at me.

"We could use a little bit more of these kinds of foreshadows, you know."

"I wish all of them were this useful," I agreed. *And a lot less unnerving.*

"All right, please take out your textbooks, we've got no time to waste," Mrs. Kartley's voice penetrated my thoughts.

"Ouch!" Elora winced as she pulled her hand out of her bag.

"What was that?" I stuck my hand in her schoolbag and extracted a clothespin.

"Mom must've accidentally dropped it in there," she shrugged. "No biggie."

"It *is* a biggie." I frowned and made my way to throw it away. "Be careful."

"Sheesh, why are you so Mom-ish these days?" She rolled her eyes. "I don't need two moms, thank you."

I narrowed my eyes at her.

"Just kidding," Elora laughed. "Now sit before Sour Face throws yet another nasty comment at you."

Mrs. Kartley raised her hand for silence in the class. Sarah raised hers to speak.

Elora nudged me and pointed Sarah's way. "*This should be good,*" she mouthed.

"Yes, Sarah?"

"Mrs. Kartley, there are students here in the class that cheated."

"Really? And who are those?"

"Elora Black and *Meghan Baker.*"

Great. Two of my enemies against me.

"And what drives you to make such an accusation, Ms. May?"

Oh, snap. She called her by her *last name.*

"When you passed out the test papers"—Sarah wore a smug look on her face as she spoke—"I saw the two of them hurriedly hide their revision sheets before you walked in and smirk as you took back the papers."

The entire class looked at us. Elora was fuming. I patted her arm to calm her down.

Well, that was *dumb.* We cheated because we "hid our sheets"? I seriously don't know what this Sarah has against me, but nothing I remember doing was worthy of her loathing.

"Well, Ms. May, I'm sure a passionate young geographer does not wish to excel in her studies using methods of such *sordidness*. Merely because they have learned to study their lessons every day does not mean they have *cheated*. Now please, Sarah, keep your claims to yourself if they will cause dispute in class, thank you."

The once-triumphant look on Sarah's face transformed completely.

"If no one else has anything to say, I'd like to begin my class, please." Mrs. Kartley eyed the class from behind her spectacles. "Good. Now turn to page two hundred eighty-six."

I scrunched my nose and did as I was told. We were just starting on Western Asia when a hard knock stopped Mrs. Kartley mid-sentence.

Without even waiting, Principal Shirley walked in, her nose in the air.

"Mrs. Kartley, I hope you don't mind if I take a few minutes from your lesson?" she asked.

"Of course not, Principal Shirley," Mrs. Kartley politely replied as she stepped away from the whiteboard and stood by the teachers' desk.

Yes, even teachers were required to call her *principal*. This is how self-absorbed she is. Come to think of it, I think she and Sarah would get along well. Or the exact opposite.

Principal Shirley stood facing us, her old wrinkles absorbing her overdone makeup. She pointed her long, manicured nail at Sarah and motioned for her to come forward.

"Uh, me?" Sarah pointed at herself, looking startled.

"Yes."

She got up and walked to the front of the class, her heeled boots breaking the pin-drop silence.

Principal Shirley set a firm hand on her shoulder and began in her hawk-like voice, "This is the best example"— Sarah's face lit up for a split second—"of a student in bad attire. This is not how you dress in school."

Sarah winced as the principal' grip tightened.

"Full-face makeup, above-knee dress, and heels."

She turned Sarah to stand facing her.

"Detention, young lady. For coming to an education facility dressed like a dancer. I will not tolerate these kinds of actions in school."

And with that, she walked out of the class and slammed the door behind her, leaving all of us in bewilderment. Sarah walked back to her desk in shame.

"Western Asia, also known as the Middle East," Mrs. Kartley began, as if nothing had happened. "An interesting combination of culture and history, attracting more than fifty million tourists annually. Meghan, can you tell us the general climate in the Middle East?"

I couldn't believe my ears. She called me Meghan. *Meghan.* My own name!

"The Middle Eastern climate is hot and dry," I began confidently. "And winters are mild, with a little rain. The coastal areas are usually humid, with a little breeze."

"Excellent answer." She gave me a small smile. "As always."

I probably looked stupid with that wide smile plastered on my face for the remainder of the lesson, but I couldn't help it. Maybe, *just maybe,* Mrs. Kartley was finally accepting me.

When the bell signaling the beginning of lunchtime rang, the class was empty within seconds.

"I need to go talk to Vanessa about something," Elora explained as we left the class (Vanessa was the head of the drama club). "I'll see you outside, 'kay?"

"Sure." I left for the yard as Elora went in the opposite direction.

I was about to push the yard door open when I heard sobbing . . . coming from an empty art classroom.

My nosy instinct urged me to go and see who was there, sitting all alone in the dark, crying to herself. Okay, it was also because I felt bad for her.

I walked in on a brunette with perfectly manicured nails, navy blue boots and an autumn dress . . . *Sarah?*

"Hey." I knocked on the door softly.

She looked up at me and scrunched up her face in disgust. "Go away," she said between sobs.

I ignored her and sat on the floor beside her.

"Congratulations, you can now go and tell everyone what a horrible fraud I am," she blurted out as she tried to compose herself. "You win."

"That's not what I plan to do at all." I hesitated, then rested my hand on her shoulder. "Is everything all right?"

"Does it look like it?" she shot back angrily as she rubbed the tears from her eyes. "I'm a mess."

I looked to face her and bit the inside of my cheeks to not laugh. Her mascara had stained all down her face and her lipstick was in a pitiful state.

"Well, you can tell me, if you feel comfortable with it," I said before I even knew it. "We can work this out."

Was it weird that I felt *bad* for her?

She just ignored me and tried to compose herself, sniffing her nose every now and then.

I sat there thinking about how worried I was about Elora. How worried I was about her, maybe leaving. And I made sure she felt loved and kept her safe.

Sarah had nobody like that. Sure, Kandice and Nicole sat with her, but it was obvious it wasn't like Elora and me.

"It's always been hard for me," she suddenly said, startling me. "You know, making friends."

I didn't know how to reply to that.

"When I finally began fitting in in eighth grade, I moved. And now I'm stuck here," she continued. "I figured the best way to draw people to me was by appearing amazing and the perfect friend to have."

"I think you went about it the wrong way," I commented.

"I know that now. But what other way is there? How will *anybody* want to hang out with a regular new girl who just moved from another city? They don't know anything about me and they have perfectly no reason to sit with me."

I looked at her in disbelief. "Well, you can actually *talk* to people. They don't know anything because you haven't *told* them. Find somebody with a common interest and strike up a conversation. It's a starter."

She sighed and set her face on her knees.

"Listen, I can understand the way you thought it'd go," I proceeded. "But I think you were a little bit . . ."

"Mean?"

"Yeah. And I guess that's what . . . kind of . . . drove people away. You should try being nice and honest; just not *brutally* honest."

"Seriously?" She looked at me in awe. "It's too simple."

"Exactly! Simplicity is the key, take it from me. I'm a person used to overcomplicating things, and let me tell you, it rarely turns out well."

"So, all I have to do is . . . talk?"

"Yes."

"Just like that?"

"Exactly."

She sat in silence, contemplating what I said.

"But what if nobody forgives me?" she whispered.

"Everybody deserves a second chance," I comforted her. "Now go make some *real* friends."

"Now?"

"No, next year."

She rolled her eyes. "Looking like *this*? No way."

"I've got the solution," I smiled. I hopped up and got some wipes from Mrs. Reyna's desk drawer and handed them to her. "These should be able to help."

She got up and went over to the window, using her reflection to erase the out-of-place makeup. After she was done, she took several deep breaths before tossing away the wipes and heading for the door.

"You know, just because we had this little conversation, doesn't mean we're . . . *friends* now," she said before leaving the classroom. "But thank you," I heard her whisper once she stepped into the hallway.

I just felt happy I could help her change, hopefully for the better.

15 PRODUCTION DATE

I told Elora everything on our way back to class.

"Well, I guess some people are stubborn, no matter how hard you try," she shrugged once I was done telling my tale.

"I guessed so too," I nodded as we filed back into class. "But it seemed like she *really* intended to change. Just . . . give her a chance?"

"Well, if you believe so, I'm in," she shrugged as she pushed our classroom door open.

Sarah gave me a particularly evil glare when I walked in, then proceeded to talk with . . . *Jennifer*. Odd; she was teasing her just last week, right?

That's a start, I told myself as I sat down.

"Good morning, students!" Mrs. Avery chirped as she

walked into class. "Please take out your writing booklets and turn to chapter twenty-two. Today, we will be discussing argumentative essays," she began once the class quieted down. "You should know the basics, since you've studied them in, well, every grade ever."

I *loathed* writing. But I did my best at it because I liked Ms. Avery. I guess that's the case with every subject, right?

"Now, argumentative essays are based mainly on facts and—" She was cut off by a knock on the door.

"Come in."

Mrs. Amena, the high school deputy principal, opened the door and apologized.

"Sorry to interrupt, Mrs. Avery, but I believe Meghan Baker is in this class?" Mrs. Amena said as she stepped in.

My heart leapt. I raised my hand in response.

"Meghan, please pack up your things. Your brother is outside." She was smiling, so it couldn't be a family emergency.

"Lucky you," Elora whispered as I passed her. *Score!* Early dismissal—every student's favorite phenomenon of their school days. I secretly stuck my tongue out at Olivia when she turned to look at me. As I picked up my bag and headed to the door, Mrs. Avery winked.

I smiled back and followed Mrs. Amena out into the hallway.

"Meghan, dear, do you happen to know which class Elora Black is in?" she asked me once the door was shut.

"Yeah, she's in there too," I replied in confusion. Why would she want—*YES!*

"So sorry, Mrs. Avery, but can I have Elora Black as well?" The deputy principal opened the door once more. "She's leaving too," she stated, only her head visible to the class.

I smirked at my friends from behind our deputy principal and flashed Lora a thumbs up. Why did it feel good to be singled out like this? I don't know; probably knowing they were jealous of how you get to skip the remainder of the day—including nasty Mrs. McAllister.

Elora subtly fist-bumped the air and hurriedly packed her things, the rest of the class eyeing her enviously.

"I have work to attend to, but you two just go out to your families, okay?" Mrs. Amena instructed as Elora got out of the class and shut the door behind her.

"Sure will." I gave her a thumbs up. She smiled sweetly before high-heeling to her office in the opposite direction and we began walking towards the exit.

"What are the odds that we're *both* being dismissed early?" Elora laughed as we neared the entrance.

"Too near," I replied mock-seriously. "Something's up. Maybe a plotted *murder*."

Then my weird sense of humor sent a shiver down my spine. *No murders. No deaths. No nothing.*

Michael's sedan (or Dad's ex-sedan, however you want to refer to it) was parked in front of Celestial High School, waiting for me.

"Look who's here!" I startled Mike as I walked up to his open window.

"About time," he huffed and sat upright. "Hop in, something big is coming."

"'Kay." I waved at Elora and got into the front seat. I looked at my brother in confusion as he tapped away on his phone. I looked at Elora, an eyebrow raised. She just shrugged.

"So? What are you waiting for?" he asked Elora as she stood on the sidewalk, scanning the street.

"Uh, waiting for my ride?"

"This *is* your ride."

See? I knew this was no coincidence.

"Why did you give us the honor of leaving early, elder brother?" I asked as Elora got in and we drove off, the school sliding out of view.

"You're about to find out," he mysteriously replied.

"Just tell us!" Elora whined.

"You'll find out in a few minutes!"

"Why won't you tell us?" I "hmphed" and crossed my arms.

"Because you'll do your lame girl stuff," he explained. "And be all like 'eek' and 'oh my God, I can't believe it!'" He mimicked a high-pitched, supposedly "girl" voice.

"We do *not* talk like that!" I objected.

"Yes, you do."

"No, we don't," Elora and I insisted simultaneously.

"Yes, you do!"

"No, we *do not*."

"Yes, you *do*!"

"No, we *don't*!"

"Please, you girls tend to have a ton of drama in your lives." He rolled his eyes.

"Oh really?" I tried to look innocent. "Like when?"

His face formed an evil grin. "Like last time you guys fought? That was *lame*."

"What was lame?" Elora looked seriously baffled.

"When you guys fought because *Meghan* was friends with *Riley*." He used his mock girl-voice once more.

My face turned a crimson shade of red; mainly because I was embarrassed, partly because I was angry.

"That does *not* qualify as an example," I insisted.

"Oh yeah?" Michael looked sideways at me. "Then what does it qualify as? Implausible argument?"

"No, I had the right to be mad; she was hiding stuff from me!" Elora argued.

"She got mad for what I saw was a feeble excuse; that's why I didn't talk to her," I added.

"Yeah, yeah, keep telling yourself that." He waved his hand dismissively.

"What?" I shrieked. "No, this was a *perfectly normal* reason to fight! Everybody fights. You don't have to suddenly judge us for it."

Elora was simultaneously stating her share of the argument. "Imagine that *your* best friend was holding out on you; wouldn't you be annoyed? It was frustrating because she vented to someone that wasn't me."

"Okay, okay," he raised his voice over ours. "I get it, it was exasperating, whatever you say. Still, it was no reason to shed tears and give each other the silent treatment."

I looked out the window to hide my reddening cheeks. I might have believed he was right, but no way was I ever going to admit it and give him the satisfaction of being right.

"In our defense, we are teenage girls. We are most likely to have this kind of behavior," I said.

"Besides, we have hormones to deal with. Sheesh, haven't *you* been a teenager?" Elora added.

"Fine." He rolled his eyes. "But I'm still not convinced."

I opened my mouth to argue but decided better not to. I had nothing to say. Females plus teen years equals disaster anyway. At least that's how my dad puts it.

"We have arrived," he announced as our house came into view. "You might wanna get into the house now. You don't wanna miss it."

"Miss what?" My eyes widened as I hurriedly unbuckled my seat belt and left my bag in the car, dashing into the house, Elora following suit.

I walked in on an empty living room and noises from . . . *my bedroom?*

I followed the voices and saw Mom sitting on the floor nearest the bathroom, and a not-so-pleasant view beside her.

I gagged a bit but couldn't help letting out a silent squeal and dancing on my toes. I sat down beside Mom, a little bit reluctant. Okay, *very reluctant.*

"She showed signs of delivery this morning," Mom whispered as she pulled me into a hug. "I thought you might want to witness it."

"Yeah." I scrunched my nose. "I do. It's just a little . . . kind of . . . revolting a bit?"

Mom laughed quietly, careful not to disturb Candy. "I expected you to say that. It's all right; I can stay with her.

You can take intervals between here and downstairs."

"Thanks." I planted a kiss on her cheek and watched for a bit. It wasn't until I got up to leave that I noticed Elora beside me, looking (surprisingly) immensely interested.

"I'll go get a snack." I excused myself as Mom and Elora began whispering about what to do.

"Gross, isn't it?" Mike laughed from his seat at the counter.

"No." I tried to figure out what to say. "Just a bit . . . unusual, that's all."

"Please, it's nauseating. I can't believe cats *eat* the—"

"Stop! Please!" I shrieked before he went any further. "Okay, it's nauseating, I admit it. But *must you* talk about it?"

"Ugh, *fine*." He got up and made his way to the living room. "It's kinda rude though, that your own *daughter* is giving birth and you're here, snacking."

"She's not m—" I sighed as I followed him. "Never mind."

***

The next few hours were made up of Mom googling how to help Candy, Elora going back and forth to get supplies, Mike lounging for no specific reason, me sneaking peeks at Candy (and hiding before I got too grossed-out), and Dad yelling "*WHAT?*" whenever I reminded him that a living mammal was in labor in my room.

Around noon, Elora came downstairs to call me.

"What?" I asked her as she grabbed my wrist and tugged me upstairs. She, being the mysterious/philosophical/nature-loving one, remained silent.

I walked in and saw five newborn kittens, each nursing from its tired-looking mom.

I overlooked the . . . *stomach-churning* mess and patted Candy gently on her head; she purred loudly in response. I got a bit less scared and sat cross-legged beside her, gazing at the five little beauties before me.

I recognized the black and ginger ones as Oreo and Caramel, and frankly, they do look like their namesakes.

I felt pretty emotional at that time. Elora and Mom probably were, too. I mean, they were there for all four hours. Maha was even more hyped than usual when she came home.

We spent probably another four hours looking at the li'l cuties and cleaning up after Candy. I decided to name the grey, white, and tabby ones Cinderella, Coconut, and Tabigail, respectively. (Mike came up with the last one.)

The rest of the day was purr-fect (pun intended). I didn't think I'd ever be unhappy after the cuteness overload I was faced with. I mean, five new baby kittens? I was gonna be a busy mom at fourteen, finding them all good homes.

All of us were fussing over the newborns; Mom insisted she call my cousins and tell them. I (after Elora's "consent") texted Riley and sent her a shot of the five furry jellybeans. The kittens were in the limelight of the household; Lora's sisters included (Mom insisted they come over.) Nobody mentioned anything other than the newborns until Elora got a text from an unknown number.

UNKNOWN: Dear Elora Black,

You have been nominated by our team to proceed to the final auditions for *Foreign*. Please drop by the Town Convention Center this Friday for the final auditions at 6 PM.

Of course, she was squealing and dancing all around the house. Mom and Dad were happy for her too, not to mention Maha, Mike, me, and most of her sisters (it was a pretty crowded house.)

It was all fun and games until I got ready for bed and realized it . . .

The audition.

16 LIGHTS, CAMERA

Elora told nobody about the audition at school. Why? You guessed it—the element of surprise.

When Friday came along, I wasn't prepared; neither mentally nor physically.

"Come *on*, Meghan," Elora urged from my doorway, dressed all warm for the outside weather. "The convention center is twenty minutes away. If we leave now we'll *barely* make it."

"I can't move," I groaned from my bed. "I'm literally dying right now."

"Please? It's my first real audition. It'd be great if you were there."

I pondered that for a while. "Of course."

I forced myself up and got dressed in nearly three layers

of clothes. I was already cold indoors; how was I going to be outside?

We barely made it in time, and Elora couldn't have been more nervous. We headed to the reception table where a middle-aged woman sat, tapping away on a tablet.

"Hello!" Elora began cheerfully. "I'm Elora Black; I'm here for the audition?"

The lady looked up at us, then back at the tablet. Elora looked at me in confusion, to which I replied with an equally confused shrug.

"Um, excuse me?" she hesitantly tried again. "I got a text confirming my audition online, saying I should come here for the final—"

"I heard you the first time," she replied, her eyes still glued to the screen. "*Wait.*"

I stiffened and tried to hold back my laughter as Elora faced the other way to hide her snickering face. *What is wrong with us?*

"Here." She passed the sample script to Elora, still averting our eyes. "Waiting is to the left. The director and his assistants will be seeing you shortly."

Elora quietly took the stapled paper stack and hurriedly walked away, mainly to avoid her hearing our giggles.

"Wait." Elora stopped when what the receptionist said registered. "Did she say *director*?!"

"Yeah …?" I looked at her questioningly.

"Oh, man, this is even more pressure than it already was! What if he kicks me out the moment he sees my face? What if he thinks I don't have the talent? What if I mess up the lines? This is a major role and I've only been in 'around the corner' video shoots and school plays!" The list of worries just kept going on and on *and on*.

"Lora, calm down," I finally found the strength to say. "You're a natural. You won most likely to become an actress three times in middle school, and everyone who saw last year's play agrees. If they can't see it, then it's their loss."

"Thanks." She hugged me. "But it isn't just their loss; it's mine, too. I *need* this role, Meg. I have so many scenes, and it's my perfect chance to make my debut."

"You'll slay them." I waved my hand dismissively. "You acting not jealous all the while I spoke about Riley was on point," I smirked. I'm guessing she blushed, but if she did, she did a pretty good job hiding it.

We spent the next half-hour in the waiting hall, practicing Elora's lines.

"Have you seen Cameron?" I pretended to ask, stroking my "beard" and using the manliest voice I could muster.

"I was told not to tell." She eyed me and glared.

"What are you hiding?" I wiggled my eyebrows and

used my hair as a moustache this time.

"Who's asking?" she asked before howling with laughter. "Meghan! Take this seriously! I need practice."

"I beg to differ," I crossed my arms and sat down. "We've been practicing since we came here and I'm pretty convinced you've got this."

"There's no such thing as too much practice."

"Yes, there is," I insisted. "Don't stress too much. You'll mess up if you do."

"So you think I'll mess up?"

"Only if you let your tension overcome you."

"*Elora Black?*"

We spun towards the entrance and saw the grumpy reception lady from earlier.

"This way, please," the receptionist barely smiled and led us out of the hall and into a narrow hallway with only one door in it, labeled "*AUDITIONS*" in bold text.

"Sweetie, please wait for your turn in the waiting hall," she said when she saw me following them.

"Oh, no, I'm Elora's best friend," I explained. "I came for moral support."

"How cute," she glared as she stopped and faced me. "But no non-auditionees beyond this point. Please wait for her in the hall."

"But—"

"*Please, in the hall.*"

Elora gave me a pleading look.

"Uh, okay," I shrugged. "Good luck. You've got this." I flashed her a reassuring smile and a thumbs -up. "Don't stress."

I gave her a reassuring hug before the grumpy lady ushered her into the audition room, leaving me standing in the hallway by myself.

***

"I was nervous at first, but then I kinda got into it, ya know?" Elora chattered on our way home. I had never seen her this excited.

"They looked impressed! I mean, I could *see it* in their expressions. I think I actually nailed it!"

I rubbed my hands together to warm them—it was *freezing. Cold without snow is useless if you ask me.*

We turned down a street that sent shivers down my spine; not sure why. I had an empty feeling in the pit of my stomach . . . I couldn't put my finger on it though. I just felt . . . scared.

"You know, I did try out for a kind of big role, but since they let me go on till the end, they must've thought I was pretty good. Meghan, you're not even listening!"

"I am!" I tried to convince her. "Just a little bit cold, that's all."

"And tired," she added, and side-hugged me. "It's all right. I shouldn't have dragged you along with me anyway."

"*No way!*" I shook my head. "I wouldn't have missed it for the world. I don't want to miss my best friend making her dream come true, do I? You wanted me to be there anyway, didn't you?"

"To be honest, yes," she smiled. "I don't know what I would have done if you weren't there to keep me grounded."

The rest of her chatter faded away into the night. No matter how hard I tried, I couldn't listen. My mind was swarmed with thoughts mixed with dizziness. *Why was I so stressed-out?*

"I was nervous at first, but I think I did pretty well. The director seemed impressed." Elora grabbed my attention again. "I think I got the part though. They asked me for my phone number and email before I left. Then again, they might do that for every auditionee."

Elora was talking half to herself as I rubbed my hands together inside my hoodie's pocket, lost in my thoughts once more. We came to a crosswalk, where I stopped. But Elora kept walking.

"Lora! It's a red light for us!" I called after her.

"What?" She looked back at me.

I motioned for her to come.

"The street's empty, come on." She turned on her heel and kept walking.

"Lora, *you* come on, rules are—"

But then it hit me.

A car rounded the corner and was speeding towards us, apparently unaware of the girls ahead.

"*ELORA!*" I yelled after her, panic rising inside me.

She stopped midway and glared. "What now?"

I looked at the vehicle barreling towards us and back at my best friend.

The driver must've seen us last-minute because I could see him brake, but the ice on the road was too slippery.

I did the fastest—and probably dumbest—thing I could think of and jumped in the middle of the road in hopes of pushing both of us out of the way. I couldn't feel my stomach pain anymore. I couldn't feel the cold anymore. My entire focus was on staying alive.

I rolled out of the way as the car screeched to a halt. The layers of wool and fabric cushioned my fall as I rolled onto the sidewalk. I heard him come out of his automobile and slam his door shut.

I stayed still on the ground, my breathing heavy, my

eyes sealed shut.

I was too scared to open them and see what had happened.

17 DREAD

"Are you okay?" I heard him ask.

"I think so," I whispered, shaking. I was terrified. I didn't want to look. I didn't want to sit up. I didn't want to find out what would happen next.

He helped stand me up and guided me to the nearest bench as I felt cold tears unconsciously trickle down my cheek.

"It's okay, you don't have to cry."

I quickly wiped my wet face.

"Where's your friend?"

I couldn't reply. I sat, frozen, on the icy bench, dreading what was to come.

I opened my eyes to see what was he doing and saw Elora's motionless figure sprawled on the sidewalk, him approaching with hesitation, obviously dialing the ambulance.

A steady stream of tears flowed down my face. I didn't even try to stop it now. I felt my throat tighten and my stomach churn, but mostly I felt physical pain in my heart. Her silent figure just shattered me. I wept like I never had before. *I knew it was coming. I saw all of this. Then why was I so broken?*

Because she was my best friend. Because it was her I went to whenever I felt down. Because it was her who encouraged me to do things I never knew I could. Because it was her who kept me sane. Because it was her I had the best times with.

And now all of that was *gone*.

Because I was too stupid to tell her earlier. Maybe if I had warned her she would've been more careful. If I had told her, I wouldn't be where I was now.

I let myself cry. I cried alone, on a frigid bench, in the dead of night. Nothing could be heard except my silent weeping and a distant howl of ambulance sirens.

Memories of what we did together flashed in my mind, filling me with even more regret and sorrow. The cold night felt colder, the silent street dead. Happiness drained out of me like a faucet turned on to its maximum.

I was broken.

The sirens grew louder and louder, but I barely heard them. I barely heard *anything*. I didn't want to open my eyes again. I was terrified . . . terrified of reality.

"Can you walk?" he asked, startling me.

I nodded heavily and used him as a crutch to get into the back of the ambulance.

"You seem fine, but we'll take you to the hospital for a checkup, okay?" the paramedic on the ambulance told me more than she was asking.

I let them sit me down and buried my face in my hands. I handed them my phone when they said they wanted to call my parents, and the rest was a blur. I couldn't think. I didn't *want* to. I just wanted to go back to yesterday, back to last week, back to when it was another normal day where Elora was . . . here.

In about no time we were in the ER, my family and Elora's already there. The nurses prevented my parents from seeing me until I was checked out by a doctor.

I had to really pay attention after that. They led me to a hospital room and gave me tests to walk, lift things, stand, sit . . . Just a few things to make sure I was fine.

"Look *here*, Meghan." The doctor snapped his fingers in my face. "I know you're confused and tired, but we need to make sure you're functioning properly."

I sighed and vigorously shook my head. "Okay." My

eyes were red and puffy; my face a mess, frozen in a state of shock; my body rigid. I felt like a robot, doing what I was asked, and my brain just . . . temporarily shut down.

"What letters do you see?"

"Uh, V?

"Good. This?"

"E."

"This?"

"O, P, C."

"You're all set." He smiled at me as he ticked a few things off his clipboard. "I'll just keep you in overnight to make sure you're okay, then you're free to go!"

He opened the door and left, and no sooner than he did so, my entire family walked in.

Mom was the first to squeeze me between her arms and babble about how glad she was I was okay. I hugged her back and for the first time tonight, I felt a little warm inside. I hugged her harder and let a few tears escape my eyes.

She sat me down on the hospital bed and ordered me to rest.

"You need it; you're tired and all worn out," she insisted before she left with Dad to get us dinner from my favorite—Johnny Rockets.

"What is it with you and accidents, young lady?" Mike

laughed.

I smiled weakly, barely visible, and hugged my knees, flashes of Elora's unmoving body on the sidewalk. I fought with myself to forget it, but what use is it to try and forget what has already happened?

"Hey, you okay, Meg?" Mike asked, a concerned look on his face.

"Yeah." Maha got up and sat next to me. "You look sad."

"Just . . ." I shrugged. I wanted to ask where Elora was, but couldn't bring myself to do it. I didn't want to face reality yet. What was Mike gonna say? *Sorry, Meg, your best friend ever is dead. Why didn't you tell me you saw it?*

A soft knock on the door made me look up. Mike got up to answer the door and walked out to talk to whoever it was.

"Meg? It's the guy who almost ran you over." He stuck his head in, a small smile on his face. "He says he wants to apologize."

I nodded in response.

When he walked in, I wanted to strangle him. I felt the urge to jump at him and choke him until he turned blue. I felt . . . *angry*. I wanted to *kill* him. If I wasn't so tired I probably would've lashed out at him the moment he walked in.

It was all his fault, my brain kept telling me. *He's the reason Elora's dead. He should be dead instead.* Even more tears stung my eyes as I fought to hold them back. A mix of anger and sadness was brewing in my limbs.

"Hey, I'm sorry." He was visibly shaking. "I tried braking but the ice was too slick and I kinda lost control—"

"It's all *your fault!*" I couldn't stop myself from screaming. "If you actually were careful we'd all be fine!" I felt tears sting my eyes and drop onto the bed. "We would've been okay if it wasn't for *you!*"

He looked startled; Mike even more so. My brother just shrugged and whispered something along the lines of "she's just tired" into his ear.

"No thanks to you, I'm now stuck in this hospital bed," I agitatedly added. "And—" I couldn't say it, so instead I hugged my knees and sobbed once more.

He looked at the floor and sighed. "I don't expect you to forgive me, but I hope you understand I really am sorry."

"It's all right." Mike put his arm on the guy's shoulder. "It was just an accident."

My eyes bulged at Mike. Just an accident? *Just an accident?* Something like this and *it's all right?*

"Well, I uh"—he pointed at the door—"better get going. Sorry again."

And he walked out.

I looked at Mike, an indignant fire rising inside me. All right? *All right?*

"I'll go get your stuff from the reception area." Mike motioned for Maha to follow him. "You need time to yourself. Gather your thoughts."

Before he left, he gave me one last hug and walked out, Maha's palm in his. When I arranged my train of thought, it was too late to yell at him, too. I was alone and groggy in a hospital room. Simultaneously, I heard nurses talking on the other side of the curtain about "bringing in the other patient." *Great, a shared room. Exactly what I need.*

I snuggled beneath the hospital blankets and pretended to be asleep until they left. Then I let my silent tears once more create a small puddle on my pillow.

I couldn't even say goodbye, I sadly thought. *I didn't say anything. This is all my fault.*

I probably mourned for what was barely five minutes before I fell into a long, weary sleep.

***

"It's been a rough experience."

"She's all right, I expect."

I woke up to a bunch of voices chattering beside me. The sun's rays penetrated the window, casting a golden portrait on my bed and onto the floor.

I stirred and sat up, shielding my eyes from the light.

"About time!" Mike joked as he brought the bed table. "Breakfast is served, m'lady."

He set the tray of stale hospital food in front of me. I scrunched up my nose in disgust.

"I thought that might be your reaction." Dad conjured a bag from under his seat. "So, we got you this."

He replaced the musty tray with IHOP takeout and gave me a hug. "You're okay, sweetie."

Of course. Mike surely told them how off I was last night. All the same, they were my family, and they loved me. I should be grateful.

I ate my waffles in silence and barely listened as they talked about God knows what. I looked at Mom and Dad, laughing on the couch. I looked at Mike, smiling too. I looked at Maha and how she was babbling on about something or other.

It made me feel a small sense of warmth. I never really appreciated these people and all they'd done for me. I never appreciated anyone. I was really lucky to have them, and it wasn't until now that I realized how I should feel a bit more grateful for the people I have in my life.

As soon as I was done, Mom and Dad got up to talk over something with the hospital and Mike went to show Maha the fountain at the center of the building.

I sighed and grabbed my phone from the bedside table.

A million notifications from every messaging app I have. I curiously opened my messages and was bombarded with what looked like this:

PENNY: OMG! So glad you're okay xxx

OLIVIA: I'm coming over. Need to see u

TALIA: DOUBLE WARRIOR! CXX

RILEY: Mike told me. R u ok?

SARAH: I'm glad you're fine.

I stared at the last one in awe. *Sarah?* A searing pain suddenly caused my head to throb, causing me to set the phone back down. I felt the bed swim under me and felt dizzy. I laid down slowly, sighing heavily. I stared up at the ceiling, a million more thoughts and memories obscuring my vision.

I thought of all the times Elora and I used to ditch math class and instead help Mrs. Reyna decorate the school. When she'd cry in the dead of night and I'd sneak over to her house for moral support. When we'd pull off the best pranks on our siblings. When we'd go out for ice cream every Sunday.

I tried to restrain myself from tearing up. I felt pathetic, crying every two seconds. *But wasn't it worth crying over?* Wasn't it worth being sad after you've lost your closest friend?

Wasn't it worth regretting everything when your literal second half is gone?

No more days where her laugh would cheer me up. No more lame inside jokes we'd laugh over amidst class. No more midnight rant sessions. No more feats in the city park. *No more Elora Meredith Black.*

She was my better half. I remembered last night. I remembered how I jumped in the middle of the road. Stupid, right? Yet it did nothing. Here I was, sitting, not a scar on my body. But Elora?

I couldn't think about it. A lump formed in my throat as I recalled the last thing she said to me; *what now?* Those were her last words to me. I was a nuisance to her moments before she left. I was the last person she saw and I was *horrible*.

She was an amazing person. She cared about and wanted the best for everyone. A small smile crept on my sad face as I remembered all the silly sleepovers and bizarre shenanigans. Three years that had been the best with her by my side.

What would I tell everyone? That I'm the reason a very important person in all of our lives is gone? I could've done something—no, I *should've* done something. Instead, I kept quiet. *Stupid, stupid Meghan.*

"Meghan?"

A whisper made me jump out of my skin. I sat bolt

upright, my eyes nervously scanning the room.

"Meg? You there?"

The hoarse, nearly quiet whisper broke out again. I slowly got off the bed and slipped my feet into the hospital slippers. I quickly wiped my reddened eyes and wet cheeks to minimize the evidence that I was crying.

"*Meghan?*"

I turned at the curtain and looked hesitantly at it. My hospital roomie knew who I was and wanted to socialize. *Not in the mood*, I thought. I'm over here wishing I could disappear and forget reality for a moment and somebody is trying to befriend me.

The *last* thing I needed.

I was going to pull the curtain open when the person on the other side pulled it before me, almost knocking me over.

"Hey! Why didn't you reply?"

She stood there, the familiar, mischievous smile on her face, her red waves falling perfectly on her shoulders, her soothing voice that could convince me to do anything.

I was struck.

"Uh, you okay?"

I was awed. I was shocked. I was brimming with joy. There she stood, in all her flesh and blood, completely alive.

I attacked her with the tightest hug I ever gave in my life.

"You're *alive*," I couldn't help breathing with relief. "*You're alive.*"

I let my tears escape me again as I hugged her even tighter, my heartbeat racing. *She's still here.*

"I'm alive? What do you mean?" Elora pushed me and looked at me in confusion. "Why wouldn't I be?"

"It's just the accident . . . and I didn't see you . . . you weren't moving . . ." I stammered. My brain and I had never been more relieved or confused in our entire lives.

"Are you *sure* that's it?" she asked me, an eyebrow raised.

"*Well . . .*"

I probably had a too high-pitched voice because she squinted at me; plus the fact that I was crying like crazy, my eyes helplessly red again and my cheeks wet.

"I may or may not have had a foreshadow of the car accident last night—"

"And you assumed we'd die?"

"Not exactly . . ."

"*Meghan*, what are you not telling me?"

I leaned against the wall, sliding down until I was sitting on the floor. Elora sat next to me and wrapped her arm around my shoulders.

"Then I kept getting . . . foreshadows," I began between sniffs. I was still crying. "Of me mourning the . . . the loss of a close one . . . so . . ." I closed my eyes and sighed, my nose stinging.

She fell silent for a while. "You assumed I was going to die," she said in a whisper-like tone.

"Kind of."

We sat in silence for a few more moments; me trying to control my crying—and failing.

"Why didn't you tell me?" she finally said. I noticed her eyes gleaming with tears in them.

"I was afraid that I'd worry you, or you'd get too circumspect, stuff like that."

"So, you kept it between you and yourself?"

"And pretty much let it drive me crazy."

"*So that's why* you were being extra Mom-ish?"

"Basically."

She hugged me once again. I hugged her back and felt myself go warm again. I was so grateful I could feel that hug for many more days to come. I was thankful that last night wasn't the last after all. That what I'd been worrying over wasn't real after all.

"Next time something like this happens, *tell me please*,"

Elora insisted.

"I will." I managed a laugh.

"Yeah, like you *totally* told me about your visions." She rolled her eyes.

"What? I only did it twice."

"Twice could be lethal."

"Okay, okay, I promise I'll try and tell you everything from now on."

"*Try?* Miss, you are very much obligated to do so."

I doubled over in laughter as she too giggled a little. My face felt tight from the dried-up tears residing on it from a few moments ago, but I barely felt it. The relief flooding me from Elora's presence was the biggest emotion I felt right now. I noticed a tiny cast on her left ring and middle finger.

"What happened?" I asked, my tone serious once again.

"Oh, this?" She held it up for me to see. "Just broken fingers. Doctor said it should heal in three to four weeks."

"How is all of you okay except your fingers?"

"Well, my thick winter outfit pretty much shielded most of me, but my fingers were bent all the way back and—"

"Okay! No need to go any further!" I stopped her. "You know stuff like that peeves me."

I sat cross-legged on the floor and leaned my head

back, covering my face with my hands. *She's okay. She's fine. It wasn't my fault that—nothing is wrong. We're all right.*

I recalled her motionless figure right after the . . . near accident.

"By the way, why weren't you moving? I mean, right after the car slipping and—"

"I was knocked out for a while." She shrugged. "But I was fine."

I thought about it for a while. Why hadn't I just asked Mike how Elora was? He could've saved me a ton of crying. Then again, I wouldn't have learned to *really* appreciate the people in my life. Particularly my family and exceptionally awesome best friend.

"Have you seen Dan?" Elora asked, snapping me out of my thoughts.

"Who?"

"You know, the guy who was driving the car?"

"Oh, yeah." I felt guilty about being so mad at him and, well, yelling at his face. It wasn't his fault the road was too icy.

Wait. Icy?

I ran to the window and saw a soft white enveloping our town. Small orbs of fluff descending from above, creating a beautiful, giant snow globe.

I was so caught up in my thoughts that it *snowed* without me noticing.

"It's snowing," I breathed onto the glass, my breath condensing on the window.

"Oh my God." Elora stood beside me. "It's beautiful."

"He came over and apologized," I abruptly continued. "I kinda made a fool of myself; *may or may have not* yelled at his face."

"*What* did you do?!" Elora sat on my hospital bed and doubled over in laughter. "Is it because—"

"Yes," I abruptly replied. Just because we avoided the situation doesn't mean I was okay with talking about it.

"Just got his driver's license," she added. "I hope his parents don't ban him from driving anytime soon."

"Me too." I sat cross-legged on my bed, facing her. "It's been a crazy twenty-four hours, don't you think?"

"Think? That's a *fact*," Elora laughed. "Well, another story to tell our grandchildren."

"Coolest grandmas ever."

I looked at her staring out the window. The golden sunlight drowning the room looked a lot more cheerful now that I knew my best friend wasn't dead. That she was by my side once again.

"I'm just glad you're alive," I sighed with a smile.

"I'm glad I'm alive too. I would've missed my body. And you, of course."

18 SOUR SWEET

Elora and I were released in the afternoon. I'd almost forgotten about the kittens, which was why I was sort of surprised when I saw five tiny cats playing on my bed.

"How are you now, my little kittens?" I asked them as I sat down on the edge of the bed. They shrank away at first, but when they saw their mom on my lap, they were a little bit more welcoming.

Lora and I barely saw each other until school resumed. Olivia was disappointed she didn't get to see us before the new week began. Talia was ecstatic, and kept barreling on about how we "defied death." Penny was such a mom about it, and the rest of the class was fighting over signing Elora's teeny finger cast.

"*Celestial's survivor,*" Talia read aloud as she wrote in tiny handwriting with a pink Sharpie on Elora's bandaged finger.

"Keep it as a memoir after you remove it," Penny suggested.

"Ew, no way!" Elora shook her head. "I don't want worms and bacteria in my bedroom, thank you very much."

I saw Sarah look at us from the far end of the class, uncertainty visible on her face. Why was she so hesitant about talking to me? Was it because of when I caught her crying? Or was it because she genuinely loathed me for something I didn't know I did?

Oh wait. *The Grammy incident.* Yeah, I *might* have been a little bit *too* mean. Maybe as mean as her. I winced at the thought and promised myself to never do it again.

"Good morning, students!" Mrs. Avery interrupted our overexcited chatter and set her messenger bag on the teacher's desk.

We all fell silent and scampered back to our seats.

"I heard that two students of ours have defied death?" She grinned and raised an eyebrow, Talia smirking in our direction.

"Do you mind?" she asked Elora as she took a red pen from her pocket.

"No, go ahead," Elora smiled, and handed over her tiny cast for Mrs. Avery to sign.

"Today we will resume reading our novel. Please open to chapter eighteen."

***

Elora was the talk of every conversation for the next week. *Everyone* wanted to add their minuscule drawing or signature until all that was seen was a scribble of colors and letters.

During lunch, Liz and her friends came up to us and they, too, insisted on adding their etching to the mix; Liz, in addition, expressing her gratefulness that we were all right.

When I passed by our class window after recess, I had a glimpse of golden gift bags on each desk. I saw Olivia and Lily opening theirs and inspecting the contents.

My eyes darted to my desk and I felt a bit of disappointment to see it empty. Every desk in class—except mine. I tried to hide my dispiritedness by joining in on the excitement of others.

"Meg, look!" Elora showed me the golden invitation card. "Sarah invited *us* to her *birthday party*. I know she's filthy rich so this is gonna be *awesome*."

Her face fell when she saw my invitation-less desk. I shrugged in response.

"No biggie." I brushed it off. "I'm cool with it." *That* was a lie.

"No." Elora set the invite back on her desk. "If you're not going, *I'm definitely* not showing my face."

"Lora, it's okay," I smiled, and poked her. "You should

go. *Have fun.*"

"I'm not gonna have fun without you," she insisted as she stuffed the invite and all the goodies accompanying it back into the bag.

"Meg." Heather tapped me on the shoulder. "Sarah wants to talk to you."

I looked at where she was pointing and saw Sarah by the class doorway, motioning for me to come.

"If she does anything, signal me and I'll come." Elora squinted at her as I made my way across the class to talk to her.

"Hey!" I cheerfully greeted her as we stepped outside the class. I hid the fact that I wanted to glare like I never did before and walk away.

"Hey." She seemed a lot less . . . made up. And more modest in the way she dressed.

"Cool, fresh look, by the way." I complimented her light winter makeup. "Decent job laying off that mascara."

She laughed, obviously in relief. Why? No clue.

"Hey, I'm having my birthday party in a couple of weeks—" she began nervously.

"Yeah, I saw the bags." I gestured at the door of nine-2 behind me. *Why did she want to talk to me about this?*

"So, I know I've been very . . . mean, and handed out a

bit . . . cruel comments . . . to you."

"A bit?" I raised my eyebrow jokingly.

"Okay, a lot," she laughed. "But I wanted to apologize. I didn't see that you were just trying to be nice back in the art room. So, I was kind of hoping you'd forgive me . . . and maybe come to my party?"

She pulled another golden bag from behind her back. Okay, so she wanted to give it to me *herself*. That was . . . oddly nice.

I felt suspicious towards her sudden pleasant behavior, but I decided to push that aside . . . for now.

"Of course!" I took the bag and hugged her warmly. I mean, hugs make everything better, right?

"Thanks," she smiled. Wow, that new makeup really *did* suit her!

"How's making friends coming along?" I asked to break the awkward silence.

"It's *wonderful*," she began, her excitement growing. "That fandom idea; genius! I found four other girls that are in the Skeleton Clique!" she squealed.

"Nice!" I nodded in amazement. Sarah? A *Twenty One Pilots* fan? Didn't see that coming.

"Oh, and Jennifer has read the *entire* Percy Jackson series, too! Like, we have *so much* in common."

Looks like I barely knew her. Or . . .

"Sarah, were you changing yourself?" I asked. "At the beginning of the year?"

She wore a puzzled expression. "What do you mean?"

"I mean, look at you now." I tried to find the words. "You dress differently, and you're into things that when you first came seemed like too uncool for you."

"Yeah." She bit her lip. "I thought I was going to be made fun of for the fandoms I'm in, so I pretended to be the basic teenage girl."

"Figures," I laughed and thankfully, she did too. "Well, basic is boring. Be *unique*. Be *you*."

"Girls, get in class please."

We turned to see Mrs. Reyna standing behind us.

"Uh, don't we have geography?" I asked.

"Yes, but Mrs. Kartley is busy at the moment. I'm your substitute!"

Sarah and I looked at each other in awe. *Score!*

"Come on in now, I have some things in store!" She smiled pleasantly as she ushered us into class.

I took my place once again beside Elora and showed her my gift bag.

"Wow, personal delivery." Elora nodded in approval.

"Not bad."

"So? Are you going?" I asked in mock ignorance.

"I don't know . . ." She stroked her invisible beard in thought. "There's this certain girl, Meghan Baker. I don't really like her."

"Oh yeah." I scrunched up my nose in disgust. "She's the *worst* human you could ever meet."

We fell silent for a second or two before doubling over in laughter.

It was great to have my best friend again. Except this time, I didn't have to worry about Death dropping by to visit.

19 YET TO COME

I was way more relaxed now that the worries of the car crash had faded over the next few days; even Mike had noticed.

I walked in after school to Michael lounging on the couch, flipping through the TV channels.

"Why are you so lazy, mister?" I suspiciously raised my eyebrow as I hung up my coat and scarf.

"It's for science." He rolled his eyes. "Where's Elora?"

"Her place. I was gonna go there after I dropped off my stuff here."

I was making my way to my room before Mike intervened.

"Hold it!"

I hesitated and slowly spun on my heel. "What is it?"

"Come," he motioned with his finger.

I obeyed and walked over to where he was sitting.

"Sit."

"I'm not a puppy."

"*Sit*."

I did as I was told and took a seat beside him.

"Why were you so off lately?" He squinted at me in a questioning manner.

"What do you mean?" *He's definitely on to me.*

"Before this weekend, you were all tense and distressed; constantly. The past couple of days you seem a lot more nonchalant. Explain."

"What? There were just a few things in school . . . projects, exams, you know—"

"You had a foreshadow, didn't you?"

I fell silent for a moment. There was no use lying now.

"*Well*, I may have seen the accident a few weeks ago, and kept getting visions of me mourning the loss of a 'she,' so I kind of assumed . . ."

"Elora would . . .?"

I hesitated a bit. "Pretty much."

He looked at me through squinted eyes for a few moments. It creeped me out. Then he sighed heavily and hugged me tightly, taking me by surprise.

"Meghan, I told you. A few seconds of the future should not define your present."

I hugged him back and breathed out gratefully.

"I'm glad I have a brother like you."

"Yeah, I'm glad I have me too."

I couldn't help giggling. He was pretty awesome . . . though slightly irritating at times.

"Well? I need to finish my research. How long do you plan on staying here?"

I laughed and resumed my path to my bedroom.

"Good luck on your research, Dr. Michaelstein," I called after him as I sprinted up the stairs.

In no time, I had changed and was knocking on the Blacks' front door.

Mrs. Black opened the door. "Meghan! Come in, come in."

She gave me a tight hug before ushering me in. Her house was by far the noisiest on the block. With Elora having three older sisters and younger twin sisters, it was bound to be chaotic.

I made my way across the frenzied living room and up

the stairs to Elora's bedroom. I pushed the door open to see her on her desk chair, her legs propped up on her desktop.

"You're lucky your house is filled with sounds," I commented for the billionth time.

"You keep saying that," she replied, her eyes still glued to her screen. "Try switching for a day and we'll see what you think."

"I'd *love* it," I insisted, flinging my handbag onto her bed and tossing myself beside it.

"Sure." She set her phone on the table and sat cross-legged on the chair. "You seem a lot more . . . chillaxed, am I right?"

"Well, I don't have to worry about the murder of my best friend." I sat up to look at her, a wide smile on my face. I could finally hang out with her normally; without having to make sure all danger was at bay.

"Yeah," she nodded slowly. Then she looked at me hesitantly, as if she was unsure if she should say it or not.

"Elora, what is it?"

"It'll still happen."

"What'll still happen?"

"You know . . ." She shrugged. "The visions of you . . . in grief and all."

"So you're saying . . . someone's *still* gonna die?"

"I don't know, it's just a guess."

I sat in thought for a while. Maybe I didn't change fate. Maybe the near accident was completely unrelated to me in lament. Could make sense. And someone was *still* in danger!

"Good job spoiling my mood like that." I rolled my eyes and threw myself back on her bed.

"I should be honest," she shrugged. "It's my job to give you the truth when nobody else will; whether you like it or not."

I stared at the ceiling, a frown on my face.

"No use sitting here and worrying about what's still yet to come." Elora jumped up and pulled me up with her.

"But you know I will."

"Don't think about it," she urged. "What'll happen, will happen. Besides, we don't know how far away these foreshadows are."

I kept silent.

"Listen, I overheard Talia and the others discussing going skating in the park this afternoon; why don't we join them? Just relax a little . . . and forget your foreshadows."

"Okay." I thought about it for a while. "It is harmless to have a little fun."

"Good, because we would've gone whether you wanted to or not." She rummaged inside her shoe closet and extracted her old coral ice skates.

"I don't have skates!" I realized when Elora headed for the door.

"Really?" She raised her eyebrow at me. "*That's* your excuse? You could at least try harder."

"No, I really don't. They're too small so we gave them away."

"Then aren't we lucky Skylar shares our shoe size?"

***

"MEGHAN! Over here!"

On the far edge of the otherwise deserted rink, Talia, Olivia, Leah, Alex, Penny, June, and Jessica were waving at us.

"Did you overhear it was a small gathering or a park party?" I joked as I sat on the snowy bench to put on my skates.

"I didn't expect all of them to be here either." Elora shrugged as she joined me on the bench.

I saw the group slip and slide across the frozen ice to get to where Elora and I were tying up our skates.

"Hey!" Olivia hugged me in welcome. "We didn't know you were coming!"

"Last-minute change of plans," Elora responded casually.

"How cool is it that it's *snowing* again?" Talia twirled on the ice. "Makes up for last year's snowless winter."

"Cold without snow is a waste," June agreed as she followed Talia and Alex onto the ice.

"That's *exactly* what I thought!" I agreed as the rest of us joined them.

"What's up with Sarah's party?" Jessica called over the scraping of skates and sudden outburst of music throughout the park.

"Oooh, gossip." Leah skated over to Jessica.

"It's *not* gossip." Jessica rolled her eyes. "I'm just curious why she's had a sudden change of heart . . . being all nice."

"It *is* suspicious," Alex nodded slowly. "Do you think she's up to something?"

"Oh, *I* know," June piped up. "She's being nice so she can lure us into her house and give us a slow, painful death as she sucks our *blood*."

"For the millionth time, June," Penny shook her head. "Sarah's *not* a vampire."

"She might be," June shrugged.

"No, but Jess has a point," Leah began, obviously thirsty for something interesting. "Why did she change suddenly? Why is she hanging out with Jennifer? When did all of this happen?"

"Calm down, Sherlock." Elora shook her head in disbelief. "Maybe she realized she was a pain to everyone and decided to give herself a fix-up."

"I'm not buying it." Leah crossed her arms. "What about you, Meg? What do you think?"

I froze as they all stared at me. Was I supposed to remain loyal to my promise to Sarah, stay silent and brush it off? Or sell her out and tell them what really happened?

"Maybe she found the right kind of friends, that's all," I shrugged. "Come on, let's not waste time talking nonsense. Mom will want me home soon and we didn't even *start* to enjoy our afternoon."

***

"Now, try gliding backwards," Talia instructed me. "But on an outside edge."

For the sixth time, I did as I was told. She insisted on teaching me the *axel*, or whatever it's called.

"Good," she nodded in amusement. "Now do it again, but try to turn afterwards."

"*What?*" I looked at her in disbelief. "Talia, I *cannot* do that."

"You won't get hurt," she assured me. "Just give it a shot."

"*Your* ambition is to be a figure skater, not mine."

She looked a little hurt, which made me regret the words as soon as I had said them.

"Okay, I'll give it a shot," I gave in. She clapped her hands in glee and led me to an unoccupied space on the ice.

"Now, *skate*."

I took a quick mental picture of the scene before I began skating backwards.

"Good, now try leaning outwards a bit," I heard her instruct from behind me.

I tried extending my leg before the sky darkened into a sunset-y purple. But I wasn't skating; I was sitting on the grass in a full-skirt dress, looking at the crowded rink.

"I've seen this," I whispered. "I've seen it all. Which makes it a hundred times more terrifying."

The person next to me shuffled their feet, then hesitantly sat down beside me.

"Are you okay?" Elora's voice asked me.

"Okay?" I shook my head in disbelief. "It can't be. I mean, there must've been something I could have done."

"Meg, I'm . . ." Elora sat in silence. "I'm sorry. It must hurt so much."

"It does, doesn't it?" I looked wistfully at the tens of people; laughing, joking. "She didn't deserve it. She didn't deserve any of it. If only I had paid more attention, she would still be here . . ."

My voice trailed off as my view slowly transformed into the afternoon.

"Meg? Are you okay?"

Elora's face was inches from mine, visibly worried. The rest of the gang was huddled around me, looks between awe and concern drawn on their faces.

I took a quick look at the situation and realized what had happened: I spaced out while I was skating and crashed. I'm guessing the no response from me got them worried.

"Uh . . ." I looked from one expectant face to the other, baffled. *What* was that vision? I struggled to search my brain for a proper excuse, but my brain was stuck on the foreshadow.

"Yeah, I'm fine," I lied. "Just got a little bit too into it."

"Are you *sure*?" Leah asked. "You totally zoned out for a few seconds there."

"Got a bit lost in my thoughts, that's all," I shrugged as Elora helped me up.

"Meghan, it's as if you were *completely* not there," June argued. "Are you one hundred percent certain there's nothing you need to tell us?"

"Nope, I'm good." I gave Elora a pleading look.

"You seem a bit off lately," Penny added.

"Nope, I am me! Perfectly normal." I widened my eyes at Elora. "Fresh air is all I need, you know?"

"Huh?" Elora looked at me in confusion.

"To keep my mind off stress," I added, subtly jerking my head in the direction of home, or away from the park at least.

"*Oh*," Elora finally understood. "Uh, would you look at the time! Six already? We really need to be getting home."

"Mom wanted us to help her with that thing, yeah," I smacked my forehead and made my way across the ice. "The, uh . . . meeting . . . with the women from . . . yeah."

"Sorry, guys, we're gonna have to bail." Elora waved as she followed me. "See you at school!"

As I waved goodbye, their faces didn't seem convinced at all.

"Are you sure you're good?" Olivia yelled after me.

"One hundred percent!" I cupped my hands like a megaphone. "Sleep deprivation; that's all."

"All right!" Olivia yelled back. I could see their faces loosen up a bit. "Get some rest, okay?"

"Sure will, Mama Olivia," I laughed, and followed Elora to the bench of earlier.

"We really need to control your foreshadows," Elora thought out loud as she untied her skates and put on her sneakers. "They keep getting you into trouble."

"The girls are onto me," I agreed. "Thanks for covering up for that. Not that it did any good, though."

"Hmph! I *saved* your behind!"

"They still look skeptical."

"What did you see, anyway?"

I sighed heavily as we began our walk back home, my breath condensing into a small puff of chilly air.

"I'd rather not say."

"*Meghan.*"

"I know, I know. But this was just like the others. Still talking about who's gonna . . . leave."

"How about we do a movie night at my place?" Elora suggested. "*That'll* free up your mind a bit."

"What if I get a foreshadow mid-movie? What will I tell your parents? Sisters?"

"I'll cover for you," she assured me. "But you *need* this break. To stop overthinking the future."

"Okay, I'll give it a shot." I sighed again, unconvinced. But there was no arguing with Elora.

20 TRENDSETTER

I felt a lot better the next morning. I hadn't had any visions since the rink incident, and the crisp, morning air was doing me good.

"Meghan!" Talia ran up to me as soon as Elora and I approached the high school entrance. "How are you feeling?"

"A lot better," I smiled. "Nothing a good movie can't fix."

"We know what's going on." Olivia looked at me gravely.

"Uh, what?" I played dumb. There's no way they found out about the foreshadows . . . is there?

"You're stressing over Sarah's party!" Penny jumped in. "Because you're enemies and all. You're not sure if you should show up or not, after the tension between you two."

"They're not *enemies*," Talia pointed out. "Just . . . not-so-good friends."

"You know, I think you're right," I nodded slowly. *Phew. Still safe.* "What *should* I do?"

"I think you should *totally* come," Elora played along. "You know, it'll be like a white flag."

"They were never at war," Olivia laughed. "But I think you should come too."

"Okay." I pretended to think. "Sure. I'm coming."

"Yes!" Elora pumped her fist in the air and high-fived Talia.

"We'll see you in assembly." Elora waved at them as we walked away and towards our good ol' classroom.

"Don't be *too* enthusiastic of an actress," I commented once we were out of their earshot. "They might get suspicious."

"Excuse you, who's the potential actress here?" Elora replied with a smirk.

After hurriedly dropping our belongings in class, we went back outside and joined our class line.

"My goodness, look at Sarah," I heard Leah whisper behind me.

I spun around and saw Sarah walking towards our class

line up, chatting with Jennifer.

"What's wrong with her?" I nudged Elora.

"Her *shirt*." Elora looked just as awestruck as the rest . . . of the *school*. Everybody everywhere was whispering, pointing, laughing.

I paid closer attention and saw her wearing . . . *a skeleton clique t-shirt?*

Nobody had *ever* worn a fandom tee in school—at least not after Lara Thompson, *the* most *fashionable* and closest-thing-to-celebrity girl, said it was "uncool" back in 2011. She singled out a girl for wearing a Sailor Moon graphic tee (not in a good way though.) After that, the *entire* school hadn't ever worn their fandoms publicly, *ever*.

Since then, anyone who has ever worn a fandom t-shirt was considered an inferior outcast.

"Uh, Sarah," I saw June approach her nervously. "You're not supposed to wear that. You know, there's this thing—"

"Oh, I know about Lara." Sarah waved her hand dismissively. "I *chose* to wear it."

"Okay . . ." June looked at her like she was *crazy*, then slowly walked away.

"*She's mental*," Olivia mouthed to us as she slipped in line.

I saw Sarah cover her distressed expression by talking

with Jennifer as they lined up behind me.

"Cool shirt," I complimented her.

"You think so?" Her face lit up.

I nodded in response. "It's a bit . . . contrasting, but I like it."

"Thanks," she smiled, and blushed a little.

I smiled back and looked to the front where the principal was taking her place in front of us. Frankly, I was weirded out by her decision too, but no need to make her feel even worse about it, right? Not after how she was dealing with the beginning of the year.

All throughout the day, most of the girls were whispering about *how on earth* Sarah's fashion choice took a swift turn—from Zoella-worthy to graphic tees. I caught her a few times hiding her face between pages of her textbook or blush crimson red whenever a giggle broke out in class.

But it didn't end there.

During lunch, everywhere around the school were people pointing at her and snickering behind her back as she walked alongside Jennifer. Awed and surprised faces followed her, some even pitiful and disdainful. She buried her red face between the pages of her novel and quickly walked past.

"I *cannot* believe her," Elora whispered when she passed by our usual spot.

"Me neither," Olivia agreed. "Seriously, *what* is she thinking?"

Well, Lana had been a fashion legend and it was a big "don't" to disobey her. On the other hand, though, she'd dealt with enough hate before. Of course, I thought it was ridiculous that she wore that, but who am I to judge? It's her choice, right?

"Guys," Penny frowned. "It's her freedom to choose what she wants to wear."

"Yeah, but *this?*" Talia scoffed. "It's *dreadful.*"

"Come *on*," Penny objected firmly. "Don't make fun of her."

"We're *not*," Elora replied just as steadfastly. "We're just judging her fashion choice."

"That isn't so nice either, is it?" Penny crossed her arms. Elora wasn't the only one with a strong personality.

"People like us make her feel insecure. Why do we have to be so mean? She wants to wear it, so be it. She isn't doing us any harm. Why should we make her feel bad about her preferences?"

Everybody fell silent. Frankly, I was even surprised myself. Penny was usually the "go" kind of person who was up for whatever the group was up to. It wasn't like her to go against the flow like that.

Not that there was anything wrong with it.

"Come on." She got up and brushed off her pants. "I've got something to fix. Who's coming?"

We all sat in uncomfortable silence as she looked from each face to the next, determination in her eyes. I bit my lip and pretended to be interested in the grass. I couldn't bring myself to look at her.

"Nobody?" she asked. "Fine. I'm still going."

"Wait." I accidentally found myself saying it without even intending to. *Oh well, might as well just do it.* "I'm coming."

She grinned and hauled me up from the ground. She strode off into the school building, me trailing behind.

"Where are we going?" I asked.

"To find Sarah."

"Why?"

"She's going about it all wrong."

"About what?"

"About making a change."

I didn't understand what she was up to but went along with her anyway. She spotted Sarah slip inside the bathroom, visibly ashamed.

We caught up quickly and walked in after her. Lucky for us, it was empty.

"Hey, girl!" Penny cheerfully greeted her.

"Oh, hi." She looked startled, and somewhat nervous.

"So, I've noticed you're a bit . . . stressed-out?" Penny winked.

Sarah couldn't help laughing. "Yeah."

"What for? The shirt?"

"Kind of . . . Jenny told me about the Lara thing, but I had no idea it was *this* intense."

"What made you wear it?" I asked. *Curiosity killed the cat, Meghan. Shut up. But satisfaction brought it back, right?*

"Well, I thought I'd make some friends," she shrugged. "I mean, if I saw someone wearing a Twenty One Pilots shirt at the mall I would've struck up a conversation right away. Meghan told me that would work, too."

"Oh." I felt a twinge of guilt. So I was the reason she was being shamed at school. *Ouch.*

"Your idea's brilliant!" Penny began. "It's just that . . . the *execution* of your plan needs a bit of tweaking."

Sarah sighed heavily and closed her novel. "What do I do? Wear a hoodie?"

"Not at all." Penny put her arm around her. "The key is *confidence*. The thing is, you're walking while hiding your face, minimizing your talking," she explained. "It makes you *look* irresolute."

"*But* if you walked tall and behave like you usually do, it'll *make* others want to do what you're doing," I joined in. "Shamelessly loving your fandom. You'll make them want to *be* you; confident about what you love, careless of what the world has to say about it."

"You think so?" Sarah still looked hesitant.

"Nuh, uh, uh." Penny wagged her finger at Sarah. "I said *confidence*. Pretend nobody's looking; it'll be easier."

Sarah sighed and straightened her back, wearing the most authentic smile she could manage. "How about this?"

"Perfect," Penny smiled. "Now go make others *want* to be you."

She walked back out, leaving Penny and me with a satisfactory feeling.

"She just needs company," Penny piped up. "You know, to make her . . . less lonely."

"True," I agreed. "Maybe begin with *us* being her friends?"

"You can check that off." Penny stood deep in thought. "Oh, I've got it! How about we *all* wear fandom shirts!"

"It'll be like she began a trend!" I was excited. It meant I could wear all the fandom hoodies I wanted to as well. *And they're a lot.*

I've wanted to do that ever since . . . ever! Maybe now's

209

the time.

"*Everyone* will catch up soon. Man, aren't I a genius?" Penny grinned in triumph.

Unfortunately, when it came down to telling the rest, it didn't seem like such a genius idea. We gathered our gang in class minutes before lunch ended to talk it over.

"Are you *crazy*?" Elora's eyes almost fell out of her head when Penny proposed her idea. "No way! I'm not risking my fashion reputation!"

"*Please*," Penny persuaded them. "It'll be good for *all* of us."

"She does propose a compelling argument," Olivia agreed. "We'll all be able to wear what we like to."

"I'm not risking my reputation either!" Leah shrieked. "No way!"

"Let me get this straight," Alex joined in. "It means I can freely wear my Supernatural merch, right?"

"Accurately," I replied.

"Perfect! Count me in," she smiled as she leaned back in her chair.

"Do I *have* to?" Elora whined.

"*Yes*," I insisted. "You even get to wear your Slytherin shirt if you want."

"Tempting offer." She thought about it for a while.

"So, we have a deal?" Penny took charge once more.

Murmurs of agreement spread around the class.

"I said, *do we have a deal?*" she insisted.

"Yes! Yes, okay?" Leah replied irritably. "We're in."

"Good. Now tell all of your friends from all grades; we need to change this stupid fashion law."

***

The next day was just as Penny and I imagined. A dozen or so more girls were sporting their own favorite bands and shows around school.

The highlight of my day was when a few girls from eleventh grade (led by Bree—the next-gen Lana) thought they were "cool" by singling us out. They were dressed in all Mean Girls-y outfits so I wasn't all that surprised.

"Uh, what do you think *you're* wearing?" Bree came up to us during lunch, wearing a revolted look.

"Clothes?" Elora replied. "You use them to cover your body. You should try it, seeing you're always in crop tops and shorts."

"Ouch," Olivia laughed as Bree stormed away, red-faced, and tailed by her cronies. "Someone give her some ice!"

"Elora; the girl afraid of no one," I grinned as she performed a triumphant hair flip.

"Beware, the beauty guru is out to get you," Penny whispered, sending us into fits of laughter.

But that was just the beginning. The following day, it was an explosion of fan bases.

The look on Sarah's face when she saw all of it was great. And seeing people from different classes talk was even greater.

You could see a bunch of ninth-grade girls fangirling over Harry Potter with eleventh-graders. Doctor Who fans complimenting each other's shirts; Selenators squealing their heads off over new merch; Gravity Falls fans discussing theories; it was beautiful.

Art was another story—the sketches on display for the next few days were all anime, Star Wars, Marvel, Pokémon, Disney—or, if you may, fan art, mostly.

You could even hear choruses of "Treat You Better," "Blood, Sweat and Tears," "Shape of You," "Side to Side," "Thriller," God the list goes on and on!

Not to mention the drastic fashion statement change. Not only did girls wear their fandoms, but also wore what they felt comfortable in.

From hoodies to exotic hairstyles, nobody was either judge-y or nervous about what to wear. A particular girl in sweatpants made me wish I was as comfortable as her to show up like that.

It was amazing. For the first time in a while (I'm guessing since 2011), there weren't any barriers between grades. No walls of communication between ninth- and twelfth-graders. Everybody was talking with everyone.

Who knew fandoms could be such a beautiful thing?

Celestial High was never better. Over the next few days, the teachers gradually started joining in. From Michael Jackson to the Spice Girls, everybody embraced their inner fangirl.

Or at least that's how Talia put it, right after Mrs. Greene walked out with the NSYNC logo on her messenger bag.

"If Lara saw us she would *die*," Jessica laughed. "Who was she to say fandoms were lame, anyway?"

"Apparently a show-off we all fell for," Elora shrugged. "But I'm glad that's changed."

"All thanks to Sarah!" June raised her voice for the entire class to hear. "Three cheers for the fandom-freer!"

Sarah's cheeks went scarlet, but for a good reason this time. Cheers erupted from every corner of the class. We barely even noticed Ms. Avery at the door cheering alongside us.

"Excellent job, Sarah!" she drew our attention. "You should never be ashamed of what you like. So, in honor of Sarah's achievement, today's writing topic will be something you've probably done a million times online. I want you to persuade me to join your fandom."

My mouth dropped in surprise. She seriously assigned us *that*? The real question was *which* fandom I had to pick. *Sometimes liking too many things can be annoying. Like picking a favorite.*

Everybody was ecstatic. The forty minutes flew by and before I knew it, we were getting ready to head home.

I packed my stuff and handed Ms. Avery my paper before turning to leave.

"Meghan? Can I speak to you for a second?" Ms. Avery called me.

"Uh, of course." I hesitated before turning back and standing before her desk. Elora motioned at me that she'd be waiting by the cafeteria.

"Have a seat," she instructed me. I did as I was told.

"Meghan, are you all right?"

"Yeah! Why wouldn't I be?"

"You're not concentrating like you used to."

Oops; my foreshadows.

"What do you mean?" I tried to act casual.

"Is there anything going on I should know about? Any problems . . . friend conflicts? I can help."

She looked at me kindly. I knew she was genuine; I knew she really wanted to help. But Mike told me not to tell a living soul . . .

"Yep, I'm good. Just a little bit . . . sleep deprived."

"Okay then, stop spending the late hours of the night on Twitter, young lady."

"Okay, I won't," I laughed. "If you promise not to either."

"Deal," she grinned as I firmly shook her hand and left for the day.

There was a new trend at Celestial School, and it was the best trend ever set: being yourself.

21 HAPPY BIRTHDAY!

The days leading up to a big party or event are always the best. Every second, I'd be a second closer to whatever event or party I was looking forward to.

In this case, it was Sarah's birthday. And I was a hundred times more nervouscited.

"Nervous *what?*" Mike laughed when I told him.

"You know, nervouscited. Nervous, but excited," I explained.

About every dress I owned was on my bed; every shoe on the floor; every purse where it positively wasn't supposed to be. The little kittens had fun maneuvering between my askew clothes, Candy looking disapprovingly from the corner. *What a mom.*

"Well, you should cut the nervous part," he said. "You

look perfect."

I looked at my reflection; a black-and-white, full-skirt dress with matching sling-backs and styled-to-perfection brunette curls. I looked good, but not good enough.

"You don't understand," I began. "She's *really* rich; I have a high standard to live up to. They're the *crème de la crème*. It's *huge*."

"Whether you're up to their standards or not, you still look breathtaking," a comforting voice told me.

I turned and saw a tired-looking Dad standing in the doorway, a smile on his face.

"Thanks, Dad." I found my way around my messy floor and gave him a hug.

"See? Don't worry about a thing," Mike assured me as he got up and joined our group hug. "You're going to *slay.*"

"Thank you," I giggled. "Let me just go get my coat and Sarah's gift, then we'll go get Elora."

"Speaking of coats"—Dad disappeared down the hall—"I found this in your mom's closet, and thought you might wanna see it."

He reappeared and held up a jet-black faux fur coat, perfect for any '80s star to wear.

"A soft, silk lining on the inside, smooth on your skin," he demonstrated. "And a furry outside to show off how breathtaking you look."

Breathtaking was the accurate word to describe it.

"Dad, I *love* it!" I clapped my hands in glee. "I promise to return it in tip-top shape."

"Return it?" he asked as he helped me put it on. "I did a bit of negotiating myself and it's yours to keep."

"My goodness, *seriously*?" I couldn't help squealing. "Thank you, thank you, *thank you*!"

I gave him the tightest hug I could manage.

"You're welcome, sweetie," he replied in a choked voice.

"Now come on, you'll be late," Mike laughed, and led me down the stairs.

"Mademoiselle." He bowed as he opened the front door.

"Thank you, kind sir." I bowed back and high-heeled outside, the cold air chilling my legs.

"May I escort you to your friend's house?" He held out his arm.

"You may," I giggled as I slipped my arm through his.

We walked across the street, nothing disturbing the silence except my heels and the whistling of the wind.

"Your destination is on your front." He stopped at the Blacks' doorstep. "Have fun."

"Thanks." I paused before hugging him tightly. "You're a great big brother, you know that?"

"Yeah, I get that a lot," he said with pouted lips. "I'll pick you up from Sarah's mansion at midnight, correct?"

I nodded while ringing the doorbell. An overly excited Elora opened the door, out of breath.

"Good! You're here." Her eyes glowed with eagerness. "Hey, Mike!" She gave him a small wave before pulling me inside and closing the door behind me.

"Looking good, girl," I complimented her black ensemble.

"Feeling good, girl!" she exclaimed with a little shimmy. "I can't *wait*. *SKYLAR!* We're ready!"

She paused for a moment and analyzed me head to toe.

"Do I know you?" she laughed. "*Love* the fur. Vintage?"

"Yep."

"Yeah, I'm *totally* not jealous," she grinned as she wore her white leather winter coat. She headed to the door, but hesitated and stood in front of their hall mirror instead. She took out the makeup in her purse and inspected herself closely. "Ugh, my lipstick's fading already. And now that I look closely, my eyeliner's all wrong."

She hastily touched up her highlight and reapplied her red lipstick, grumbling in the process.

"Easy on the red," I said, grinning. "You don't want to look like Cheryl Blossom."

She gave me an intense eye roll before stuffing it all back in her bag and fluffing her hair.

"Let's go!" Skylar appeared from the kitchen and grabbed her coat. "Into the car, ladies."

Elora grabbed her gift for Sarah and hurried outside, tugging me along with her.

We followed Skylar outside and got into Mr. Black's car, our heels sinking into the snow with every step.

I got in and inhaled the warm air. I felt the cold melt away from my legs and felt grateful for the warmth.

"What's this party, anyway?" Skylar asked as she started up the car. "An 'oldies but goldies' or something?"

"It's Sarah May's birthday," Elora explained. "She's having a golden-themed birthday party, and we're all supposed to wear black-and-white."

"That doesn't make sense," Skylar laughed.

"The venue, cake, her dress, and everything else will be gold," I jumped in. "We're black-and-white. To create a contrast, you know."

"Impressive," Skylar nodded. "And this Sarah girl; is she rich?"

"*Filthy*," Elora and I replied in unison.

"Which is why it's *crucial* we look good," Elora continued. "It's sure to be something totally over-the-top."

"Grab me a few party favors, will you?" She winked. "They're bound to be something big."

I never really told Elora, but Skylar was my favorite out of her sisters. It was weird how she was the oldest, yet the most fun.

We chattered on all through the ride, Elora and I unable to contain our excitement.

This was gonna be *awesome*.

"We're here!" Skylar sing-songed as we finally pulled up at a mansion.

"Thanks for the ride," Elora half-whispered. The house was even more magnificent than we had imagined.

We drove through the house gates and into the main entrance. Expensive flowers of every kind dotted the walkway. The mansion was three stories high; breathtakingly attractive. Blue ivy was beautifully overgrown on the sides, creating a beautiful contrast with the navy blue tiled roof.

If you had a dream house in mind, forget it. This is what you'd be wanting.

A guy in a black tuxedo opened the car doors for us to walk out. I looked at Elora, who looked equally stunned. Muffled music and laughter echoed across the empty yard as we got out and the guy closed the doors behind us and

Skylar drove away. We took our time walking up the elegant stairs and to the front door.

"Hey, girls!"

The voice was familiar, but the person wasn't. Talia looked stunning in her white-and-silver ensemble, her makeup making her look even more astounding.

"No fair; your mom works at a wedding boutique," Elora joked as Talia joined us.

"That's no advantage." Talia winked. "Besides, you two are *goddesses* tonight."

"Aren't I every day?" Elora responded with a duck face.

Another man in a tux opened the front door for us, the warm air and blast of music welcoming us.

I walked in and let the warm atmosphere envelop me but before I knew it, it was daytime and Sarah was standing in front of me, dressed in jeans and the shirt I bought her.

"Okay, you *sure* she's coming with Penny?" she asked, her tone ecstatic.

"Yep," I assured her as I set the shopping bags I was holding on the floor. "We have like, three hours at least before she shows up. And I told Penny to tell me when they're on their way so we have an extra warning."

"Good." Sarah nodded distractedly as she texted someone. "Now come on, everybody's in the dining room upstairs," and grabbed my wrist before dashing up the stairs.

"So we need to find a solution." Elora was now in front of me, a serious expression on her face as she whispered urgently.

"Uh, *what?*" I looked around to rebuild my focus. The warm air hit my shoulders and I realized my coat wasn't with me anymore.

"*Your foreshadows!*" she urged. "They're sure to get you in some kind of trouble one of these days."

"What happened?" I asked. "Where's my coat? Where's Talia? *What* did I miss?"

"I gave it to the guy in the tux," she explained in a whisper as she subtly pointed at the coat rack behind me. All kinds of fancy shawls and coats were hung on display. "Talia went to the bathroom, thank goodness! Or else your spacing out would've been trouble."

"Well, sorry!" I shrugged. "I'm as annoyed as you are, but I just *cannot* control it. We should bring this up to Mike soon, honestly."

"Let's go!" Talia startled me as she appeared by my side. "Where's Sarah?"

"The party is this way." The man gestured towards a large door near the end of the foyer.

The three of us strode into the backyard, anticipating what was to come. I was ready to face the cool battering of the winter wind, but none came. Instead, the piping smell of food and the blaring of music and conversing welcomed me.

I looked up and saw a glass dome surrounding the *entire backyard.* We were outdoors, but indoors. I guessed you must be *really* rich if you could afford something as luxurious as this.

"Look." I nudged Talia and pointed upwards.

"And the setting, I can't even." Elora looked awestruck as she took in the rest of the venue.

I looked around and saw golden tables dotting the place, with matching golden seats. There was a stage-like area near the left where a *huge* stack of gifts stood. All the people dotting the scene were dressed in black-and-white— and it *did* create a beautiful effect with the gold.

"Meghan! Elora! Talia!" a very excited voice snapped us out of our daze.

"You made it!" Sarah came up and hugged us. "What do you think?"

She spun so we could have a 360-degree view of her golden dress, fit for an actress to stride down a red carpet in.

"It's *gorgeous*," I commented. "By the way, *loving* the theme!"

"It was my mom's idea," she excitedly chattered. "She even arranged all of this herself."

"Well, it's definitely *something*!" Elora joined in. "Happy birthday!"

"Thank you!" she squealed, and hugged us. "But you didn't have to bring a gift, you guys!"

"Yeah, right." Talia rolled her eyes.

"Seriously," Sarah insisted. "Birthdays are about having fun, not getting lots of stuff, you know."

"Sure, whatever," Elora grinned as she handed her the gift. "Enjoy."

"Thanks," Sarah smiled back. And for once, I could actually see that her smile was sincere.

Talia and I followed suit and gave her our gifts and wished her a happy birthday.

"Look, Olivia and Penny are here!" Talia exclaimed once she caught sight of them. "Liv! Penny! We're here!"

Elora waved at them and followed Talia towards the table at which they were seated. I hesitated and stayed back, wanting to talk to Sarah individually.

"The place looks amazing, Sarah," I began, admiring the backdrop. "Your mom really has outdone herself."

"Thanks, again," she giggled. "I just hope it shows the real me, you know."

"I thought you weren't a fancy person?"

"Oh, I'm not"—Sarah shook her head—"during school. Applying makeup every morning and carefully planning your outfit every night is just too much to worry about."

"Oh my God, true. So you *are* into fashion?"

"At times, yes. Depends on the situation, mostly."

"And why are there so many people? I am *certain* this isn't just nine-2."

"It isn't; I decided to invite every friend of mine, including the ones I made in the past few days."

"Good move!" I nudged her. "You know, I'm proud of you. For not being afraid of showing your real side, even though you were nervous about it."

"I have a particular Baker to thank for that." She winked. "Now come on, we need to start this *partay*!"

Not only was it the most beautiful party ever, it was also the most fun one I have ever attended.

Alya Smith from eleventh grade had agreed to be the DJ (I had no idea she even liked music) and let me tell you, she was *wicked*.

Sarah had prepared a ton of party games; classic and new ones. It was hilarious, watching all of us in fancy dresses run around looking for clues and a treasure, or trying to balance an egg on a spoon with heels on.

Next, we all lined up for the Macarena—the highlight of the night. The group chant of "*EEEH MACARENA*!" was the best thing; even Sarah's mom laughed.

After that, we danced—*barefoot*. I mean, how can you be comfortable if your ankles are aching? We spent the entire time fangirling over our favorite singers—and meeting new friends along the way.

Then came the cake and the chorus of "Happy Birthday," the cake being equally majestic. The four layers of golden deliciousness were devoured in no time. And yes, we all had golden edible glitter on our lips afterwards.

We spent the rest of the night dancing, laughing, snapping, talking, singing, and just plain having fun.

You could say it was the best night ever. But the greatest part? Elora was there to live it with me.

It was the perfect break from my strenuous foreshadows and the not-so-worn-away shock of almost losing my better half.

22 WHAT A SHOCKER

A few hours later, all that was left were our girls; the girls of nine-2 (at least, most of us were). The once-crowded venue was now deserted except for us, sitting cross-legged and barefoot on the stage, talking over the day.

"You should've seen Shawn's face," Jennifer laughed. "His eyes almost fell out of his head when he saw what Sarah and I were helping Mrs. May set up."

"I have never seen him so awestruck before," Sarah added. "His first words were 'How did you even *manage* to rent a glass dome?!'"

"I never knew you had an older brother," I thought out loud.

"I never talk about him much." Sarah shrugged. "He's great, but sometimes—"

"A nuisance," I laughed. "Relatable."

"Thanks again, Jenny. For coming early to help and all." Sarah hugged her best friend. She never really admitted that, but it was pretty obvious.

"Don't mention it." Jennifer waved her hand dismissively as she swallowed another piece of cake.

"Next gift," Heather announced as she handed Sarah a particularly large box.

"I wonder." Sarah stroked the box. "Should I open this one?"

"Nah." Alex handed her another one. "Save the big ones for later. Check *this* one out."

An apple-sized, golden box was between Sarah's fingers. "It's from Aunt Brittney. Should I open it?"

"*YES!*"

I didn't know much about her, but according to Elora, she was the richest of them all. Sarah untied the white ribbon and lifted the lid before letting out a really huge gasp.

"What is it?" Maya sat bolt upright.

Sarah slowly lifted up a small, black rectangle for all of us to see.

"*What?*" Elora grabbed it out of her hands to get a closer look. "A *car*? Is she serious?"

"And I wondered what that red Mercedes was doing

outside." Sarah understood and laughed.

"You're still too young to *drive*!" I added.

"I know," Sarah laughed. "Aunt Brittney has always been ahead of things. She got me a diamond set when I was *eight*. Never wore it until now."

I looked at her neck and there it was; a dozen diamonds sitting on her neck, with matching earrings, bracelet, watch, and ring. Okay, I admit, there were times when I got jealous of her wealth.

"Mom's probably gonna take it," Sarah continued as she grabbed the key from Leah's hand. "Save it until I'm old enough; just like the set."

"Why don't you keep it with you?" Elora asked. "Keep it in your drawer or something."

"When Shawn got *his* car, he took it for a drive at *fourteen*," she laughed. "I don't think she's taking that risk with me."

"Well? Did he crash it?" Alex asked, curious. To be fair, we *all* were.

"He hates me mentioning it, but yes," she giggled. "Shush, he's around here somewhere and if he hears me, I'm dead. Okay, should I open another one?"

"*Yes* please," June answered. "Open mine. It's that blue-and-green one. It's nothing big, but I hope you like it."

"My goodness!" Sarah's face lit up when she opened

the box. "A Pusheen Plushie, I love it!"

She hugged June tightly before moving on to a white box with golden and silver ribbon. *Oh no,* I thought. *My gift.* I tried busying myself with my phone before she opened it so I didn't have to face her reaction.

"Oh, this one's from you, Meg!"

"Right, it is!" I smiled. "I hope you like it." *You just had to announce it in front of everyone, didn't you.*

I swallowed hard.

She opened the box and fell dead silent. *Oops, I ruined it.*

"Hey," I began. "I know it isn't much but—"

I was interrupted by a deafening squeal and a deathly tight hug from her.

"I love it! I love it! *I love it!*" She couldn't stop jumping as she took out the skeleton clique hoodie I got her, along with a tøp poster and sneakers. "These are the *best* gifts of the evening; no exaggeration. How'd you know?"

"Well, I guessed you were a hardcore Twenty One Pilots fan since that was the first thing you wore to school," I replied, feeling *really* awkward; all of the girls' eyes piercing me. "So I figured you'd like it."

"*Like it?*" Sarah's eyes were lit up with excitement. "Meghan, I *adore* it!" She gave me another tight hug before whispering, "Thank you," and immediately putting on the hoodie—over her dress! "Not wasting a single second of not wearing it." She winked.

"Well, I kinda expected you to have all the merch," I shrugged. "Since, you know . . ." *Since you're rich? Nope, not saying that out loud, not in a million years.*

"That I'm rich?" she laughed. "Mom doesn't like me being obsessed with fandoms and all, so I'm practically not allowed to even fangirl near her. This is *everything* to me, thank you!"

"It was nothing," I smiled, and hugged her again. Seriously; I got the entire set for quarter the original price in a garage sale. Ex-fans can be *pretty* useful.

We proceeded to open gifts, exchange opinions, and fangirl over relatable objects.

Until Elora's phone interrupted.

"Ugh, who is it?" I asked, annoyed. We were having a really good time. She looked quite irritated too.

"I have to get this." Her eyes widened as she identified the caller ID.

"Who is it?" I asked.

She shut me up with her hand and got up hurriedly, standing a good distance away from us.

I was about to follow her when Sarah pulled me to sit beside her and started barreling on about where she'd hang all the posters she got and asked for my opinion.

"Look at *this*." Jennifer took out a long, silk dress from a fancy gift bag, which was replied to with whistles and laughter.

I stole a few looks at Elora; she was nodding quickly, her eyes bulging with excitement.

"Let me guess, Uncle Greg?" Sarah laughed. "He always sends me outfits from Maine and Milan. Fancy, right?"

Elora came running back, squealing inaudible sentences and jumping uncontrollably in place.

"What the heck is wrong with you?" I asked, getting up. "Calm down!"

"I can't!" she squealed. "*I got the part!*"

"No. Way!" I got off the stage and stood facing her. "Are you *serious?*"

"Dead serious!" She energetically nodded and began dancing in place.

I couldn't contain my excitement either. My best friend was gonna be in a *movie*—and we were both going to meet *the Jennifer Lawrence*. Her life's *biggest* dream was about to come true and I was here to witness it.

"What's going *on?*" Sarah prompted, her face as confused as the rest of the girls'.

"A few weeks ago, Elora auditioned for a part in a really huge movie," I composed myself and explained. "And just now, she got a call confirming—"

"*I got the part!*"

We were all in a frenzy afterwards. Sarah insisted on getting more cake to celebrate Elora's "big break." Talia, Penny, Olivia, and I were barreling on about how our best friend was going to be famous. We all begged her for autographs and showered her with confetti from the floor. Sarah *did* bring cake, and we all snapped pictures with her like she was impossibly famous.

Which, undoubtedly, she will be eventually.

And Elora was having so much fun. She gave out invisible autographs and shielded her face from the paparazzi. It was the perfect ending to a perfect night.

"Where is Mademoiselle Meghan Baker?" The coat guy came up to us in the midst of celebrating.

"Uh, me." I came to face him. I felt a bit shy; I walked in looking like a goddess, and now my hair was down, feet bare, and makeup almost gone.

"Your brother awaits you at the front door."

I looked at Elora, puzzled. It wasn't midnight yet. Why was he here so early?

I followed the coat guy inside and found Michael having a small conversation with Shawn.

"It's not midnight yet," I smiled as he noticed me come in. "I'm not Cinderella, you know."

When he didn't smile back, I knew something was up. "Hey, what is it?" I asked him in a low whisper as Shawn made his way upstairs.

"We need to leave," he replied in a monotone. "I know it's early, but we *need* you."

"What? What's going on?"

"Bring Elora too," he continued, disregarding my question. "There's nobody to take her home, so she's coming with us."

"Mike, you're scaring me," I began. "What's happening?"

"Mom prefers to tell you herself," he replied, still robotic.

I decided not to ask any more questions and made my way back to the party scene.

"Hey!" Elora hauled me back on stage. "What does the Michaelstein require?"

"Uh, we need to leave," I shrugged.

"*Aw*," everybody chanted in unison.

"Can't you stay a *bit* more?" Sarah begged.

"Believe me, I want to." I hugged Sarah. "But Mike's looking really grave. I *need* to go."

"I understand." Sarah nodded knowingly. "Well, don't forget your party favors! And *please* save those stories of yours; the snaps are priceless!"

"Sure will," I laughed as I put on my heels and gathered my goodie bag(s) and purse before hugging everyone goodbye.

"See you at school!" Elora waved as we made our way back inside.

After getting our coats and settling inside Mike's car, I began getting worried again.

"Why are you so solemn?" I asked him as I put my hand on his. "Is everything okay?"

"I hope," he mumbled. I noticed a little bit of . . . sadness in his eyes.

"Guess what," Elora piped up in an attempt to lighten the gloomy mood. "I got the part!"

"Hey, congrats!" He smiled a little. "The next big superstar."

"Thanks," Elora replied from the backseat.

We fell silent afterwards. Nothing changed much. The rest of the ride was a quiet one, filled with heavy breathing and tension in the air.

Michael's phone suddenly rang.

"Yes, Mom?" he began. "Yes, they're with me. Yeah, we're really close. Actually, we're outside right now. Sure, I'll drop them off first. Sure. Mhm. Yes, love you. Okay. Yes.

Sure. *Yes.* Bye."

He put it back down before turning down a familiar street. The street I called "shopping day special," because it had all sorts of shops, cafes, corner stores, and stands lined up on both sides of the wide road.

Michael slowed down in front of the 24-hour vet clinic. "Go on, I'll park and catch up. Mom's waiting for you inside."

I didn't even question him as Elora and I stepped onto the cobbled sidewalk and walked into the warm veterinarian's shop and clinic.

Mom and Dad were in the waiting area, equally solemn expressions on their faces too.

"Mom? What's happening?"

"Doctor Sam wants to see you," Dad replied. "Elora, you stay here."

She did as she was told and took a seat next to Mom. I made my way down the familiar hallways and into Dr. Samantha Williams' office.

"Meghan!" she smiled as I walked in. "So great you could come here on such short notice. Have a seat."

She motioned to the chair set next to the examination table. I nervously obeyed and hesitantly opened my eyes. My poor feline was lying helplessly before me; her breathing heavy, her eyes dull.

"Oh, my sweet little Candy!" I couldn't help myself. I got up and hugged her, restraining a tear with difficulty.

"We're lucky she had her vaccination appointment today, or else I wouldn't have been able to see her." Dr. Sam looked me straight in the eyes, then at Candy.

"It's okay." I rubbed Candy behind her ears. "You'll be okay."

She purred softly and meowed weakly in response. She attempted to look at me, but decided it was better to just lay her head back down.

"Is she all right?" I asked Dr. Sam, almost too afraid to hear the answer. I saw it all coming. I *knew* what was gonna happen.

"I have an assumption," she confessed as she stood beside me. "But I can't diagnose it yet. It's . . . post-mortem."

I didn't need a dictionary to find out what that meant. I just held onto my softly meowing cat. I didn't want to let her go. Not yet. Not after all those years with her.

"You're *very* lucky." Dr. Sam put her hand on my shoulder. "Mike got you here just in time."

I kept rubbing her favorite spots; behind her ears, under her chin, her neck. She meowed weakly now and again, visibly fatigued. I kissed her head and held her close.

"I love you," I whispered into her ear as a single tear

wet her grey-and-white fur. "I really do, with all of my heart. I loved you more every day. Don't ever forget that. You are an amazing cat, Candy. I love you so much." And I kissed her furry head one last time.

Then the purring ceased. And so did my heartbeat.

23 RUNAWAY

The rest was a blur. I didn't listen to anything Dr. Sam was saying. I felt a bit lightheaded too.

I saw her move her lips. I saw her look at me with tear-filled eyes. I felt her hug me tight.

"Meghan?" Her voice snapped me back to consciousness. "Are you okay?"

"Uh, y-yeah," I stammered as I backed away from the examination table. "Just need . . . some . . . fresh air."

I bolted out of the room, down the hall, through the lobby and onto the street. I inhaled the cold January air and looked down the empty, snowy road.

There was only one way left to go, and that was forward.

"*Meghan!*" my mom yelled from inside.

I don't know what provoked me, why I did it; I was clueless. It was probably another dumb move from my side. I just bolted down the street, no destination set.

I didn't even feel the pain my heels were causing me. I didn't feel the thick coat stiffen my movement. I didn't feel the cold wind battering my legs. I didn't feel anything, except a tightening pain in my chest and a tense knot in my throat.

I had no idea how long I'd run for or how I got there. I ran blank-mindedly throughout the streets of our city. I couldn't think; I didn't *want* to think. I wasn't prepared.

Suddenly, I found myself standing on the road across from the park. The noisy, busy park. Where it'd be impossible that I'd be alone with my thoughts. Which was the last thing I wanted; loneliness with myself.

Perfect.

I hesitantly crossed the street before using the less-popular park entrance to get in. I followed the unfamiliar winding path until I heard squeals of laughter and chatter. Looking between the trees, I saw the ice skating rink. The rink where I had all my fun times in. The rink where I was so happy, very much like those people were right now.

The rink where I was unaware of what was to come.

I picked my way through the dry earth to a withered patch of ground littered with dead leaves and broken twigs.

Staring at the colorful scene ahead, I took off my sling-backs and sat down, observing the people in my sight, hugging my knees.

A mid-thirties woman was skating with her daughter in hand, her face embedded with a wide smile. Her daughter's face reflected her joyful expression as she babbled on.

A college student had headphones in his ears as he skated alone around the rink, visibly following the rhythm of the music his phone was setting.

An old guy was helping his wife do an awkward shuffle across the ice; Liz and her friend guiding the grandma too; the lot of them giggling.

Two middle-school sisters were practicing a routine, most probably for the skating competition to be held in a couple of weeks.

Here and there people were skating; either with their friends, family, spouses, or just on their own. But they all had one thing in common that I didn't share.

"Mind if I join you?" Elora's hoarse voice broke my train of thoughts.

"What's the use?" I shrugged.

"What are you . . . thinking about?" she tried again.

"I've seen this," I whispered. "I've seen it all. Which makes it a hundred times more terrifying."

I heard her shuffle her feet before hesitantly sitting down next to me.

"Are you okay?" she asked, concern noticeable in her voice.

"Okay?" I shook my head in disbelief. "It can't be. I mean, there must've been something I could have done."

"Meg, I'm . . ." Elora sat in silence for a moment. "I'm sorry. It must hurt so much."

"It does, doesn't it?" I didn't even look sideways. "She didn't deserve it. She didn't deserve any of it. If only I had paid more attention, she'd still be here. It's all my fault. I'm to blame. I saw it coming, yet I never bothered to ask. It's my fault; mine only."

"Meg," she sighed. I could tell she was struggling to find the right words to say. "Dr. Sam said it had no symptoms. We wouldn't have known anyway. Even the diagnosis would require a necropsy. You're *not* to blame."

"Yeah, doctors wouldn't have known." I repressed the croak fighting to leave my throat. "*But I did! I knew!* But I did nothing about it. I had the foreshadow; I had a chance, but I blew it! If only I'd paid more attention. Asked. Told Mike. We might've been able to do something! But stupid Meghan never gets anything right."

"Meghan, you're *not* stupid." Elora looked me sternly in the eyes. "You did the right thing by ignoring those visions. That's what's meant to happen; we couldn't have stopped it."

"I could've." My voice cracked. "But I didn't."

"No, you couldn't've. These foreshadows are just a glimpse of the future; we never would've known for sure. You did nothing wrong."

We sat in tranquility for a few moments before I broke the deathly silence filled with laughter.

"It hurts," I confessed, allowing a silent river of sadness to escape me. "I loved her so much."

"And I'm sure she knew." Elora hugged me and sighed. "She's gone, but she left knowing she had the best cat-mom in the world."

And that's when the waterworks began. She handed me a tissue as I cried my eyes out. I remembered how horribly I cried back at the hospital, thinking it was Elora. I hugged her and cried even more.

I didn't notice a few people slow down as they neared us, curiosity filling their faces.

The cold evening seemed even colder without Candy rubbing her warm fur against me. I felt broken; like a piece of me was taken away. She was family; we all knew that. I was overwhelmed, upset, mortified.

I was only nine. I'd been begging Mom and Dad for a cat for months. I made a presentation to convince them. I made most of my friends send my parents anonymous letters telling them to "give your daughter a cat. She is a good girl."

On my birthday, they surprised me with a 2-month-old,

grey-and-white British shorthair. I named her Rosy, then Matilda, then settled on Candy. I'd had her for five years and kept her closest to my heart.

She was my first best friend. She kept me company countless sleepless nights. She'd been by my side through the stress of middle school. She interrupted my homework and made doing it more enjoyable.

Elora insists it wasn't my fault. But I was sure there must've been something I could do. Something that would make me be at home, cuddling post-party with Candy under the bedcovers.

People without pets would call me crazy, crying over an animal. Just an animal. Well, she wasn't. No pet is. She was one of my best friends. I had this unconditional love towards her, which nobody seemed to understand.

I cried and cried as Elora hugged me on the edge of the park skating rink. I could hear her sob a little too. It was Sarah's birthday. And Candy's death day.

After I composed myself, I took the time to wipe my face from the tears (and messed-up cosmetics) before I stared back into the rink. This time, several people were staring at me.

Like I cared.

"Hey, Meg," I heard Mike's broken voice beside me. He took a seat to my left and put his arm around me.

"It's okay to feel bad," he began. "Candy was close to all of us, though I know you're the most damaged one. But I wanted to let you know we're all sad. We feel you. *I* feel you. You can cry. It's only normal. Just don't overdo it. Don't feel guilty. It's the circle of life. Just listen to Dr. Seuss. Don't cry because it's over; smile because it happened. We all had many wonderful memories with her, and we're surely making more with her next generation."

I remembered the five shorthairs back in our house and couldn't help smiling.

"Now come on," he continued. "We need to get you home. Besides, a certain five kittens expect you soon."

I stood up and wiped my face once more.

"Sheesh, you look like Godzilla with that makeup," Mike joked. "Let's get you home before somebody sees you like this."

***

The next day, we buried her in our backyard. I cried the whole time. And I saw my foreshadows come to life.

The remainder of the weekend was dull. I would stare aimlessly at her place, my heart aching. I spent most of my time with the kittens, trying to forget. But it was hard to forget a piece ripped out of your heart.

After talking it over with Mike and Maha we renamed the eldest cat, Cinderella. She's now Candy Jr.; she very much resembles her mom, anyway.

Elora came over every day. She made sure I wasn't bawling my eyes out and helped me do something else other than feel sad and soggy all day.

When the new school week came along I didn't want to go. I felt terrible. I didn't want to talk about it, which, sadly, is the thing Celestial High students are best at. With a little motivation from Mom I managed to go, but avoided all contact with any human beings. At *all*.

Needless to say, I was irritable throughout the day, but it wasn't until lunchtime that I wanted to break someone's neck.

Olivia, Penny, and Talia didn't mention Candy at all, and neither did Elora. We were (correction; *they* were. I sat in silence) talking about Dua Lipa's newest album before Nicole came along.

"I heard you lost your pet cat," she bluntly stated, a mischievous glint in her eye. "So sad. I sympathize."

I ignored her, the others awkwardly sitting in silence too.

"Such a heartbreak," she continued. "I mean, she was so close, *so close*. Like a best friend."

She looked at us, expecting some reaction. Nothing came.

"I had my own birds once," she pouted. "They died

247

because of hunger. I missed them at first, but I mean, I didn't *cry*. They're just animals."

"Everyone's different though," she sighed. "Just some of us are a bit more . . . dramatic, in presenting our feelings."

A few snickers erupted from around the yard.

"I mean, it's *so* heartbreaking, but avoiding contact with your *friends*? Now that's just—"

I wanted to jump up and knock her off her feet. But Elora did it for me.

"*Can't you prevent your lips from producing rubbish for once?*" Elora shook her head in disbelief. "I get it; you're trying to make her feel *ashamed* for *crying* that her *best friend* is gone. That's a loser move, by the way."

"I am offended!" Nicole gasped, and held her hand to her chest. "I would never!"

"Really? Then stop acting like you're a friendship expert," Elora retorted. "Because we all know your best friend is a mascara tube."

"Insulting her attitude *and* her fake lashes." Talia fist-bumped Elora after a very red-faced Nicole stormed off. "Gold move, Lora."

"Somebody's a Regina George *wannabe*," Penny whispered loud enough for the girls next to us to hear, who erupted in uncontrollable laughter with us.

And then the conversation carried on like nothing had

happened.

When lunch was over, I saw a pile of tissue paper on my desk. Only it wasn't.

I sat down and saw tens of flowers neatly sorted on my desk, notes tied to their stems. I took my time to read what they said.

She loved you; just remember we still do!

I am so sorry . . . your Candy will meet my Lily!

Candy; forever in our hearts.

A pet, a best friend, and a mom. RIP

Always loved; never forgotten <3

I looked at all the little notes and cute doodles of a grey cat with angel wings and felt immensely touched. All these girls cared about me enough to bother to do something.

They *understood* how hard it must've been to handle this. And they showed it. I looked at every girl as she filed in and smiled. Every single one was eager to make me smile.

So I did. I wasn't happy about Candy's death, that's for sure. I was just happy that we had made great memories together, and we loved each other a lot.

Moreover, I had plenty of people who loved me all

around me. I wasn't gonna let myself get so caught up in one person that I forgot the others; at least not *again*.

So, I smiled. I smiled a teary, happy smile at my friends.

"Thank you." I looked at the pile of flowers and then at my class; my *girls*. "I really do appreciate this. And I love you all so much."

Long story short, Ms. Avery walked in on a watery, extra-large group hug.

I tried to loosen up a bit as the day wore on. It was the *least* I could do after what they'd done for me.

24 A FURRY SITUATION

When I came home, I was surprisingly a lot less depressed and in a much better mood.

"Of course you are," Elora laughed when I confessed it to her. "All you needed was a good dose of love and laughter, that's all."

I skipped the front door and instead went around the house to where Candy lay beneath the ground.

"These are for you, my sweet," I smiled as I settled the assortment of flowers beside ours from last night, saving some for my bedroom.

"I love you," I whispered before heading indoors from the back door.

"Hey, honey." Mom hugged me when she saw me. "I hope today was okay."

251

"It was," I smiled, and looked at Elora. "It was better than I imagined."

"Meghan, I hope you remember our agreement on the kittens . . ." Mom hesitantly reminded me.

"Yeah, I'm okay." I flinched as I remembered. "Can I just . . . keep two instead?"

"You got it." She hugged me one more time before Elora and I headed upstairs.

"The *agreement*?" Elora asked as she scooped up Caramel in her arms.

"We kind of agreed that it was too much to have six cats in the house," I explained. "And we were gonna give away four kittens."

"Have you decided which two you're gonna keep?"

"I think so." I picked up Coconut and sat cross-legged on my bed. He had begun showing some black and orange patches of fur here and there.

"Candy, for sure." Elora picked her up as she mentioned the kitten, before gazing deeply into her eyes and smiling. "You have your mother's eyes, Candy Jr."

"So funny," I grinned as I picked up Oreo and Tabigail too.

There was a tiny pool of kittens on my bed. We spent our time doing our homework (with five furry jellybeans sitting on our books) and sneaking cookies from the kitchen.

I was tackling math when I saw Oreo at my feet meowing softly.

"Okay," I laughed as I picked her up and set her on my desk, next to Caramel and Candy.

"Hey, Lora," I finally said. "What did you get for question six?"

"X equals seven and y equals two point five," she replied from behind me.

As I wrote down the answer, Oreo began playing with my dancing pencil.

"Oh, Oreo," I sighed as I petted her tiny back. "You miss her too, don't you?"

She gave me a tiny meow in response.

"Yeah, I miss her presence too."

I fell silent for a few moments.

"I just can't help but think . . . how different it would be if she was still around. If I could still see her every day."

I backed away from the desk and spun my chair, staring at the ceiling. How different *would* it be if she was still here?

For starters, I wouldn't have come back miserable from Sarah's awesome birthday party.

I shook my head and stopped spinning, facing a concentrating Elora sitting on the carpet.

"I saw this too." I rubbed my forehead. Elora looked up from her math workbook, confused.

"A foreshadow, right?" She had that knowing look on her face. "And assumed it was . . . me."

I nodded slowly.

"You seem a lot more . . . untroubled, than a few days ago," she added. "Are you over it already?"

"I don't think I'll ever be," I admitted. "But the waterworks are sorta gone. My heart still hurts, and I'm still sad, but . . . I realize that I should just appreciate the people I *do* have first."

"Good decision," she smiled. "Well, that's life. It doesn't go the way we want it to. We just have to deal with the bumps in the road as we come across them."

"Look at you, so philosophical and deep," I laughed. "But you have a point. I just didn't want to grow up so fast. I mean, the older I get, the more I realize the world isn't what I thought it was. Instead, it's this dark, gloomy place I am probably going to get lost in."

"Not necessarily." Elora set down her books and crossed her legs. "I mean, you can make your own happiness. We will have to deal with the hard times life throws at us but remain strong. Man, I hate growing up."

"You're telling me . . ."

"As a part of growing up and facing life, pick two

kittens."

"*Now?*"

"Yes. You don't get that much time in real life. Come on, pick two."

"Okay, okay! Don't pressure me!"

I looked at the three kittens on my desk and the two by the window. They were all so cute. They were all the children of my best friend. They were all mine . . . but not for long.

"Candy Jr," I said finally. "Because she looks like Candy so much."

"And?"

"Uh . . ."

"Come on!"

"Okay." I bit my lip in guilt. "I'm so sorry you guys! But . . . Coconut."

"Choice well made." She got up and put all three kittens back on the floor.

"I feel bad!" I hugged my knees and buried my face. "The rest are gonna hate me."

"They'll forget you soon enough." Elora shrugged. "They're still kittens."

I sighed heavily. She was right. This is life. The cruel,

vicious, mercurial life I just met.

"I mean, I could stay in touch with their new owners," I added hopefully.

"That's my girl!" Elora hugged me. Then after a moment added, "Always remember to look at the bright side."

***

"Meghan! Bring the kittens downstairs; he's here!"

I sighed and looked at my three temporary kittens, sadness overwhelming me.

"One of you will leave today," I told them, fighting the urge to cry, my voice failing me. "I will miss you, but I'll always check up on you."

I opened my bedroom door and they went barreling down the stairs, closely followed by Coconut and Candy.

"Muhammed should be here any minute," Mom informed me as I followed my kittens downstairs.

It must've been obvious I was sad, because she came and hugged me tight.

"He'll take good care of whoever he chooses," she assured me. "I know his family. He's a good guy."

Our entire block knows his family. They throw the *best* summer parties every June, complete with lightsaber fights, water balloons, summer snacks, video games, and every other imaginable activity.

They were very likable, too. I trusted him, but I couldn't bring myself to let go of any one of my kittens. Not after what happened last weekend.

As the doorbell sounded, the kittens gathered by the door, eager to see who was it. To them, that sound usually meant Elora coming over, and apparently, she wasn't only *my* best friend.

"Hi, Meghan!" he cheerfully greeted me as I opened the door, careful not to let any of the furry creatures escape.

"Hey," I smiled. "Here for the cats, I suppose?"

"Yep." He bent to his knees and petted every kitten. "Aren't they angels?"

"Yeah, they are," I sighed. "Which one do you want?"

"This one." He picked up Coconut in his arms. "Reminds me of Lily, the cat I had back in second grade."

"Uh, that's not an option," I smiled feebly, and took my nearly calico kitten from his hands. "Sorry."

"Oh well." His shoulders slumped. "Can I take . . . this one?"

He pointed at Caramel. My heart ached. I looked into her green eyes as she meowed and pawed at my feet to pick her up. I felt the waterworks make their appearance but I pushed them back.

"Yeah." I put Coconut back down and picked Caramel up.

He held out his arms expectantly.

"Just . . . promise you'll take good care of her," I began. "And always keep her food bowl full. And she doesn't like the meat flavor, just the tuna one. And don't forget—"

"I know, Meghan," he laughed. "I know. I've had cats before. I still do. I'm just going to university soon and want company; the family cat stays with my parents. We are expert cat people, rest assured."

I hesitated before slowly extending my arms. He gently picked her up from my hands and held her near his chest.

"You're in good hands," he soothed her. "What's her name?"

"Oh, uh," I exhaled heavily, "Caramel."

"You know"—his face changed into a more sympathetic expression—"you can always come and visit; whenever you like."

"Thanks." I looked at the four remaining cats, then back at him. His face seemed genuine.

"Mrs. Baker," he smiled at my mom. "I'll be on my way, then."

"Thank you for taking care of her!" my mom enthusiastically replied.

I hugged her one last time before he disappeared behind the door, leaving me with one less jellybean of happiness.

25 MOVING ON

I kept smiling and tried as much as I could to keep my positivity levels high throughout the next couple of weeks, but frankly, it was hard.

I missed Caramel more and more every day. I wanted to visit her daily, but didn't want to seem like a freak. Muhammad got my number from Dad and insisted I come and see her.

So I did. It took her a moment, but she remembered me. They had three other cats, and Caramel was thoroughly enjoying her time annoying her older housemates.

My heart ached for her a little more every day.

In school, the girls were very enthusiastic about Tabigail and Oreo. A lot of them offered to take them in, but either their parents wouldn't agree or they'd be allergic.

"Thanks anyway," I laughed when Olivia offered to take them in and use a mask to not sneeze.

"At least she's with your neighbors, right?" Penny focused on being enthusiastic.

"I just hope *Nicole* doesn't offer," I shuddered. "I heard her talk to one of the girls in nine-1 that she's 'totally a cat person now' and is looking for an 'itty bitty baby kitten' to adopt."

"Say no." Talia scrunched up her nose in disgust. "She'll probably have her dead in the first week."

"*Talia!*" Elora stared at her wide-eyed.

"What? It's true." She shrugged. "She wouldn't offer anyway. She *despises* literally everyone inside this building."

"What about that cousin of yours?" Olivia suggested. "She really likes you and is likely to take really good care of them."

"She's a dog person," I snorted. "Like, who would pick *dogs* over kittens? Cats are *way* cuter."

"Excuse *you,*" Penny raised an eyebrow. "But dogs don't ignore you when you call them to come over."

And cue the heated debate over whether cats or dogs were better. Which *kind of* continued until the following lesson.

And the rest of nine-2 was split into "Team Cats" and "Team Dogs."

"What on *earth*?" Mrs. Greene walked in, awed.

"Sorry, Mrs. Greene, but it's just that *Elora* here thinks cats are *better* than dogs." Jessica rolled her eyes.

"Elora!" Mrs. Greene gasped. "Cats are *not* better than dogs."

I gaped at our physics teacher. *Wait, she literally said she loved her sister's cat last week!*

"They are better than *all* animals in general."

Team Cats was celebrating and Team Dogs was protesting, but in no time Principal Shirley was patrolling the halls and we all fell silent.

What I loved the most about going to school recently is that it kept my mind off of the recent . . . misfortunate events.

When I was at school, my friends kept me busy by laughing, playing, or just being downright mischievous.

The teachers were pretty sympathetic as well. There were a few, *rare* occasions when I'd tear up or get emotional, but those moments would get washed away as quickly as they had come.

Two weeks after Caramel's departure, a couple from the other side of town contacted Mom about . . . my two remaining kittens.

How did I find out?

I was at Elora's place, hanging out with her sisters on a normal Tuesday afternoon. We were dancing when I saw Mike arrive at our place, noticeably late, and an oddly shaped box accompanying him.

"I'll go check it out." I nudged Elora and pointed outside. "Be right back."

I hopped over to my house and snuck in, because Mike was usually so mysterious and full of surprises (and usually tried hiding his inventions from us).

I was tiptoeing upstairs when I heard Mom's laugh echo from the kitchen. I wasn't really interested until I heard her say:

"Oh, they're *darlings*. Just born; barely two months!"

I stopped and slowly turned around, making my way to the kitchen.

Pushing the door open, I stepped in and silently sat at the kitchen counter and listened intently to her conversation.

"Aw, that's so adorable. Yes, I understand. So true! So how about, say, Saturday? Perfect!"

My heartbeat quickened as she led the phone call to a close.

"Just one, right? Good, that's all we have left anyway. Goodness, no! Yes, we have everything you need. Mhm. Sure thing, sweetie. Okay. Goodbye!"

She hung up and slipped the phone in her back pocket.

"Mom?" I quivered. "Who was that?"

"Meghan!" She jumped. "I didn't see you there; at least cough next time!"

I smiled weakly as she composed her breath.

"These were the Filembans from the other side of town," she explained. "They're just married and want to adopt a family cat. Luckily, Emma, one of my friends, overheard their conversation at Applebee's and told them about your kittens."

"Wait, so you found a second family *already*?" I gasped. I was kind of hoping Oreo and Tabigail could stay a *bit* more with me.

"Yes." Mom looked at me with that "don't-get-me-started-again" look. "We agreed to keep two *only*, remember?"

I sighed heavily and nodded. "I know. Just hoped I'd stay with them a bit longer."

"Well, they promised that you can visit anytime you want," Mom assured me. "They're really nice. Tabigail will have a sweet new home."

"*Tabigail?* They chose already?"

"Well, I told them the only cat left was a tabby one—they *adored* the name, by the way—and agreed to take her in."

"*Left?* What do you mean?"

Mom laughed before looking at me straight in the eyes lovingly.

"I found a family for Oreo this morning, too. She's coming this Thursday."

***

Two days later, picture this: me, still in the morning's clothes, curled on my bed, crying my eyes out. Now picture Elora, with about a dozen chocolate bars, sitting cross-legged beside me and gently patting my head, cooing words of comfort. Picture four curious kittens, playing between the bed and the floor, eager to find out what was going on.

Then picture my family's curious faces as they pass my room. I—erm, *we*—were a mess.

"It's okay," Elora comforted me. "Let it all out."

And I let out another sob of sadness, pain, and agony. I tried to explain what I was feeling, but neither my brain nor my tears aided in that.

"Don't talk, it's fine." She waved her hand. "I get it. The next week's gonna suck. So will mine, it's all right. We're in this together."

We spent the day between crying (mostly me), devouring chocolate (mostly Elora), having our last precious moments with Oreo and Tabigail, and just staring blankly at the ceiling and wondering if life has a meaning at all.

Then we decided to change and apply a bit of makeup,

fix our hair, redo our nails, and basically refill the energy that was drained out of us.

It's a scientific fact that giving yourself a makeover and looking good is good for your health. Well, I think it is. I mean, look at me now!

Elora was just telling me about the new video Lily Singh had uploaded when Mom's voice came floating up the stairs, bringing our conversation to a halt.

"Meghan! Oreo's new owner is at the door. Could you let her in while I finish up the dishes?"

I looked at Elora with sad eyes.

"You never know," she smiled. "Just hope for the best."

I sighed and dragged my feet downstairs. Dreading what was to come, I opened the front door to welcome *my kitten's* new . . . *owner.*

But when I opened the door, I had an even bigger shock.

Mrs. Kartley was at our door.

I was unsure of how to react. My own *geography* teacher? Here to adopt *my kitten*? I was positively awestruck.

"Mrs. Kartley!" I exclaimed when I finally gathered my thoughts. "Uh, what brings you here?" *Dumb question, Meghan.*

"I believe I have a kitten here waiting for me?" She raised an eyebrow. And then, she did something I haven't seen her do since I met her; she smiled at me.

"May I come in?" she asked.

I stared at her blankly.

"Sure." I stepped aside and let her in. My mind was still fuzzy.

Elora was taking the stairs two at a time and almost tripped at the end; her face reflected my thoughts exactly.

"Have a seat!" I gestured at our living room before hurrying to where my best friend stood.

"Would you like to explain why our geography teacher is here?" she whispered urgently.

"I know just as much as you do." I shrugged.

"Melissa!" Mom exclaimed as she entered the living room. "Odd to see you out of school, isn't it?"

"*Melissa?*" Elora and I exclaimed in hushed voices.

"Her name's *Melissa Kartley?*" Elora raised an eyebrow. "Her name isn't all that menacing."

I simply shrugged and walked towards the living room.

"*Come on!*" I whispered, motioning for her to come.

"It's *your* cat, not mine." She crossed her arms.

I rolled my eyes and pulled her along with me. There

was a kind of awkward wrestle before I pushed her into the living room and walked in behind her.

"Elora," Mrs. Kartley (uh, *Melissa*?) smiled. "I shouldn't be surprised you two are together."

"Quite inseparable, the pair." She turned to Mom and laughed, and carried on with whatever conversation they were having.

Elora and I sat silently on the side and whispered whenever we found out some new information about *Melissa* Kartley.

"Meghan." Mom suddenly looked at me and snapped me out of my thoughts. "Would you go bring Oreo, please?"

I felt the tight knot in my stomach tighten even more. Smiling weakly, I got up and motioned for Elora to follow me.

My nerves tensed even more with every step I took towards my bedroom.

I opened my door carefully, making sure there were no cats behind it.

"Oreo," I called him. His tiny black head appeared from under the bed and meowed softly.

My heart nearly broke as I picked him up and stood at the doorway. I looked at Elora sadly, then at Oreo again. I was gonna miss him. A lot.

"I mean, it's not like you can't visit your teacher, right?"

Elora shrugged with a small smile.

"I love you, Oreo." I kissed his small head as he meowed in response.

I walked out and Elora closed the door behind her. We made our way downstairs, one step at a time. Mainly to spend more precious seconds with Oreo.

When I was at the door of the living room, I could feel my tears stinging, fighting to remain in my eyes.

I walked in timidly. Mrs. Kartley's face lit up when she saw the little kitten.

"It's been a while since I've seen one of those." She got up and took him gently from my arms.

"Hello there, Oreo." She held the kitten in front of her face. "How are you?"

Oreo seemed to be really comfortable and settled in her hand, meowing softly.

My heart melted. He just looked so cute. I told myself that I still had Candy and Coconut, but a part of me still wanted the other three to stay.

"You know, I understand your deep affection towards your cats," Mrs. Kartley suddenly said. "I love all twelve of mine."

Elora looked at me and smiled. Okay, so her information about the number of cats our teacher had *may* have been inaccurate.

"One of my cats recently gave birth," she continued. "But it was a litter of two kittens, and they both died. I think she wouldn't mind taking in this one as her own."

I felt kind of sad. The cat probably got over it, but it still would make her happy to have a younger one to care for. Even though she was about a couple of months old.

"Well, I'd better get going." Mrs. Kartley said her goodbyes to Mom and headed for the door.

"Take good care of him," I couldn't help saying. "I really will miss him."

"Understandable," Mrs. Kartley smiled.

And then it was my turn to do something I hadn't done since she met me either; I hugged her as tight as I could, and felt a warm teardrop escape my eyes.

She hugged me back and whispered, "I will guard him with my life. Let's just keep your newfound information about my last name a secret, okay?" She winked.

"And Meghan," she added, "I expect you to visit. You too, Elora."

Elora and I smiled to each other and then at her.

"Without a shadow of a doubt."

26 LAST BUT NOT LEAST

I felt a lot less broken-hearted after Melissa's—I mean, *Mrs. Kartley's*—visit. I realized that it's not all that bad, and maybe there were actually people out there who understood me. Other than my family, I mean.

My foreshadows this time were just typical things; school, lunch, basically normal life—however you'd like to define "normal."

Michael advised me to try and get a grip on them, so every morning I'd lay in bed for about ten minutes, trying to see a glimpse of the future. It never really had an effect.

Until the day the Filembans came.

I had woken up and was laying in my bed as usual, except it worked. I don't know how I figured it out, but I knew I was not where I woke up.

I looked down and I realized I was wearing different pajamas. The date on my phone read April 24 as well.

I was snapped back to the present by Mom standing impatiently at the doorway. I'm pretty sure it was just a coincidence, but I liked to tell myself that now I actually knew what I was doing.

"Stop acting all sleepy and get up!" she snapped. "The Filembans are here!"

I obeyed and got dressed before going downstairs to meet them, expecting the worst.

But it wasn't all that bad after all.

I couldn't help smiling as they fussed over Tabigail and looked utterly bewildered. They had brought a cat cage, cat toys, cat food . . . almost every object a cat might need.

I enjoyed sharing my experience with them and telling them all about my tabby, what she likes and how she usually behaves. I explained to them the tools they'd bought and their uses, what they'd need, and how to manage a house with a cat in it. I even recommended Dr. Samantha to them.

"Tell her that Tabigail is Candy's daughter," I smiled. "Meghan's Candy."

"Sure," Mr. Filemban smiled. "Anyway, feel free to visit us anytime!"

"Of course," I laughed. They looked kind of adorable, the way they fussed over every little detail and were very excited over adopting their first kitten.

"Seriously," his wife added. "We could use a little help with her every now and then."

"Well, you know who to call," I smiled. "Cat sitter at your service, too!"

After their visit was over I felt empty, and a little sadder. I was no longer gonna go upstairs and have five tiny, furry monsters attack me. No tiny puddles of fur. No fighting over who I should pet first.

But when I saw Coconut and Candy, I was determined to be happy with what I have and make the best of it.

Two were better than one, right?

**

"Hey!" Penny and Talia stopped me in the hallway as I was headed to class. "Listen, I know we haven't talked about it much, but how's it going?"

I raised an eyebrow at her. "How's what going?"

"You, dealing with Candy and all." She dropped her volume. "And the three kittens."

I smiled and hugged her. "Thanks for asking."

"It's my duty," she laughed. "So? Are you okay? Elora told me Tabigail left three days ago."

"The house is a bit empty," I admitted. "But I'm great. Every one of them said I could visit, so there's nothing to worry about."

"And are you coming to terms with Candy's death?" Talia piped up.

I winced at the sudden mention of the subject.

"Well, kind of," I said, almost to myself. "I'm still devastated; still feels weird not having her around. But I'm a bit . . . better."

"Wonderful news." Olivia hugged me from the back. "Now we can have the old Meghan back!"

"You can't," I suppressed a laugh. "She's dead."

We all broke into fits of laughter before Elora came along.

"What's so funny?" she insisted.

"Nothing," I giggled. "Thanks, guys. I don't know how I would've made it here without you."

"'Tis my duty!" Talia announced. "Besides, why would we be your best friends if we didn't?"

"True," I nodded thoughtfully.

"Let's not get too sappy." Elora waved her hand dismissively. "Come on, I'm starving. Where are those cupcakes you promised us, Olivia?"

***

When geography came along, Mrs. Kartley was in an

unusually good mood. And I had a good guess as to why she was so happy.

"Good morning, students," she half-smiled as she walked in. "Had a well-rested weekend, I hope?"

She began smiling more often and joking a little more. Frankly, it was the most enjoyable lesson yet. Maybe it was my mom's effect on her? I mean, Mom usually does that to people, being the social butterfly that she is.

Or maybe it was the baby cat I gave her last Thursday.

Towards the end of the lesson though, Elora was very excited. And I didn't have to wait long to find out why.

"She let me," Elora whispered in my ear.

I looked at her with a puzzled expression. I was about to ask when she answered first.

"Hey, girls!" She captured the class's attention once Mrs. Kartley left. "Did ya know Mrs. Kartley's first name is *Melissa*?"

I guess *Melissa* knew how much Elora loved being the center of attention. Everybody went wild and asked Elora how she knew; I sat in my place, smiling to myself and thinking of my two cats.

I began appreciating things more. I never really realized how lucky I was to have the people I had until now. Truly, *really felt* how important they were. And it was a good thing I did.

I never expected anybody to be as damaged as I was. But as it turns out, every member of my family had missed her.

"You know," Mike commented at dinner, "I kinda miss Candy playing with the wires as I was working. Made me feel less alone up there."

"Yeah, me too," Dad nodded. "I'd have somebody with me late at night when all of you were asleep."

Surprisingly, though, Maha was the most saddened.

"I know you're her owner and all, but I feel like she was my cat too," she commented. "How do you think Kira would feel if her goldfish died?"

"You know what, I *really* don't know," I replied. I learned that I even had to appreciate my little sister, as irritating as she is. "Fish don't really do much, do they?"

"Not really." She shrugged. "His only special talent is excreting really long strings of—"

"Okay! I get it! No need to get any more gross." I made a disgusted face as she doubled over in laughter.

I had a little quiet moment for myself that evening. Well, for a while at least.

I was on my rooftop refuge when Mike's head appeared from the window.

"Mind if I join you?" he asked.

"You're not gonna take no for an answer, are you?" I laughed.

"Nope."

He climbed up and settled down beside me.

"It's freezing up here." He blew on his hands to warm himself. "What are you doing here alone at night?"

"Trying to not think." I shrugged. "Staying away from the hubbub a bit."

"Okay, but our house is quiet anyway." He squinted at me. "I thought loneliness was the opposite of what you wanted."

"I'm watching people pass by," I explained. "Wondering what's bothering them, what major life-turning event happened, who they're missing . . ."

"So you're judging people? Not so nice."

"Oh my God." I shook my head in disbelief and laughed. *What an idiot.*

We remained in silence for a few more moments before I spoke up.

"What do you wanna talk about? We both know you came looking for me for a reason."

"Nothing specific," he replied. "Just to see how you're doing . . . Hey, how are your attempts at controlling your visions coming along?"

"Pretty good," I brightened up. "I was able to see the morning of the 24th of April."

"Nice!" He playfully poked me. "When was your last foreshadow?"

"This afternoon," I grinned.

"What was it?"

"Just your wedding, nothing big."

"*What*?!"

I laughed at his awed face. "What? It was gonna happen sooner or later, right?"

"Did you see anything relevant?"

"Nope. Except that I looked *fabulous*."

"Come on!"

"I'm serious! I just saw us talking, somewhere off to the side in the wedding venue. You were making me promise I'd still come and visit after you'd moved out."

"And you will, won't you?"

"Darling, please. You won't see a day pass without me bugging you."

"Gee, sounds comforting."

27 IT COMES NATURALLY

Another reason Mrs. Israa is the best teacher on campus: she took any chance she had to make us go out and explore biology on our own.

This time, she seized the opportunity of our otherwise "free" day to take us to the park, where we were supposed to collect samples of certain plants and . . . *insects*.

"All right, class!" she announced once we were off the school bus. "Team Plants, your list is with Jessica. Team Insects, you're with Heather. First team to collect all items required wins. Now go!"

We spread across the green expanse of land and began our hunt. Along with most of the class, we headed for the higher grounds of the park for a wider view.

"Isn't the park beautiful?" June breathed in as we reached the peak of a hill.

It really was. Green carpeted the whole of the place, patches of trees here and there, and the sound of the soft whistle of the wind.

The cool winds hadn't ceased but the snow was already melting. The once-frozen rink was now the artificial lake, filled with tiny fish and algae.

Which was why I loved Mrs. Israa's trips most of all. I *loved* studying the surroundings and taking in the beauty of everything. Still a part of geography, right?

"Remember, nature enthusiasts," Elora laughed as almost everybody paused and took in the beauty of this place, "We're here on strict school business."

"Come on, I think I saw daisies here the other day," I told Elora as I scanned the items Jessica had assigned to Elora and me.

"Well, there are blue hydrangeas over here!" Elora called over her shoulder. "No use walking there and here again."

I hurried over and saw cerulean flowers settled amongst other colors; identical to the ones Mike picked a while ago.

I felt goosebumps spread up my left arm before I rolled up the sleeve and had a second look at my once-renowned warrior *bruise*.

"Everything okay?" Elora asked when she caught me staring at my blue-and-silver bruise for a while.

"Yeah," I sighed. "Just thinking . . . how crazy life's been after a small accident."

"Well, that's life, isn't it?" Elora began.

Beware, philosophical Lora on the loose, I thought to myself, and couldn't resist laughing.

"I'm serious!" she continued. "Time is a rhythm, where even if the tiniest change is seen, it can lead to a cascade of effects downstream."

"I know for a fact you stole that from Zecora," I laughed. "Give creds! How rude."

"Whatever." She hid her smile as she picked a bunch of hydrangeas.

I stared at my arm once again. How did I still think it was beautiful? I really didn't know. It led to a crazy path, though quite interesting.

"Let's go get the daisies." I pulled down my sleeve and headed downhill.

She looked around cautiously before asking, "How are your visions, by the way? The morning practice you told me about?"

"I did it the day Tabigail left," I grinned. "I traveled to April 24."

"Awesome! What had changed?"

"It's only two months ahead! What *would* change?"

"I dunno, a lot of things." She shrugged. "Maybe a second lab accident?"

"How *dare* you even suggest such an idea!" I shoved her.

"Just kidding." She doubled over with laughter at my expression. "It'll be fine. I know it will."

"I hope so," I sighed. "The past few months have been *insane*. I'm just glad it's over."

"For now, at least," Elora corrected me. "There's gonna be more adventures. I mean, I just landed a major movie role, you have new psychic powers, and we're still freshmen. I'm pretty sure there's *lots* more to come. But we'll deal with it," she quickly added when she saw my upset face. "I'll be with you every step of the way."

"Yeah," I nodded. I just felt really lucky to have a supportive best friend and brother. Who *knows* how insane I would've gone if I hadn't told anyone.

"You know, maybe it isn't all that bad," Elora continued. "Your visions could end up being useful. Detect crime or whatever."

"I don't plan on getting a job on the police force, thank you very much." I shook my head.

"Come on, it isn't that bad!"

"Because you don't know how hard it is, *being stuck in your own mind*! Haunted by yourself. These thoughts just randomly kick in and terrorize me. It's terrible beyond words."

She fell silent for a moment. I felt bad at my sudden and pointless outburst.

"I'm sorry," she said, after a moment of hesitation. "I wouldn't know, you're right. But no matter what happens, I'm here. And so is Michael."

I smiled. "Thanks."

"Now, where are those daisies?" She came to a halt and scanned the ground for the white flowers.

"Over here." I sat cross-legged on the grass and took my time picking out the prettiest ones. "I feel bad for them," I commented. "I mean, we're just gonna experiment on them. Then they're dead."

"Sheesh, don't let vegetarians hear you," Lora joked as she sat down next to me. "That's it; we only need three. One more thing." She looked me straight in the eyes. "*Do not* let these short teasers of the future affect your present. I know you've heard it a lot from Mike but only because he *knows*. Whenever you see something that bothers you, tell us. The worst thing you could do is keep it to yourself."

"Okay," I replied. "I promise to tell you. But I can't promise the foreshadows won't bother me."

"Oh, Meghan," she sighed. "You've got this. Just stay strong."

I stood up and pulled her up with me. Except seconds later, she wasn't there.

There was smoke spreading overhead and the distant screaming of people. There were tons of individuals fleeing and the deafening sound of gunshots being released.

I was running away from where I stood, scanning the park. There was nobody I recognized. For some reason, I was running towards the cause of the commotion, where the echoing gun noises grew louder.

It was the definition of chaos.

A stranger tapped my shoulder and I spun violently.

"Come with me," his deep voice ordered me.

"*CUT!*"

A guy in a white hoodie and jeans walked up to me, slow-clapping.

"Wonderful, Lauren, *wonderful!*" he said after handing me my . . . *script?* "Second week and you're doing *great*. I knew I didn't make a mistake in hiring you. The entire board thought I was crazy, I'll give you that, but you have raw talent no other 14-year-old can come near. Great job!"

"*Meghan?*"

I swiftly turned to my right and saw Elora standing there again.

"What happened?" she asked earnestly. "A vision?"

"Yeah." I remembered the scene. "It was."

"Where? What? How?"

"I don't know." I brushed it off. "But let's not worry about that now. I'll tell you everything later. Besides, we *cannot* let Team Insects win."

We ran over to Jess, who was waving us over from the top of the hill from earlier.

"You got all of the flowers?" she asked earnestly.

"We just need roses and dandelions," I answered, checking the sheet she gave us.

"No need, I found them," she replied excitedly. "Quick! We just need jasmine and we win!"

***

"And then *what*?!" Elora's jaw dropped.

"I don't know! He called me Lauren, and said something about hiring me." I tried remembering the foreshadow from earlier.

We were on our way home for the weekend and Elora was really getting inquisitive. I squeezed my brain to remember, but a few hours had already passed by and I didn't remember to tell her about it until now.

"What else? Talk!" she urged.

"Lora, I seriously *don't know!* It was a short . . . sneak peek!"

"Lauren is my character in *Foreign*," she told herself. "Do you think …?"

"Absolutely *not*," I steadfastly replied. "Number one, I'm a *terrible* actress."

"You got the part in last year's play . . ."

"Number two, it's *your* big break! I'm not gonna ruin that for you!"

"You could've been persuaded by the money, or the fame, or whatever," she mumbled, and crossed her arms.

"No! I wouldn't! Even if I would've, now I won't. This is *your* dream, and I completely support you."

"Thanks, I think." She looked downcast.

"Hey." I went in front of her and began walking backwards. "*A few seconds of the future should not define your present.*"

She laughed so hard she had to stop walking. "Don't use my own advice against me."

"Listen to your own advice, woman," I laughed as I stepped back beside her. "It'll be fine. Plus, Mike probably has a better explanation than we do."

28 FORESHADOWED

I finished up my homework in a matter of minutes and spent the rest of the day in Mike's lab. We spent the rest of the afternoon working on something we hadn't mentioned in months . . .

The Time Explorer 3000.

I arranged all the blown-off parts and fried wires in boxes and stacked them neatly near the far end because "who knows, we might need them for reference!"

We detached the burnt plates and noted what new parts he had to order—and the budget we had was *way* low.

We (mostly he) looked over the tons of folders of analysis he'd collected and tried to identify the reason why the machine malfunctioned.

No results.

Around sunset, Mike was more miserable than after the accident itself. To be fair, though, the ton of broken debris was demoralizing for both of us.

"You seem upset." I broke the silence when he tossed another research folder onto his desk and buried his face in his hands.

"This is hopeless," he murmured between his fingers.

"Yeah." I shrugged. "Hopeless if you stop and give up. But we've got to keep trying. I didn't come up here and spend hours with you for the past I don't know how many months for you to give up. God, you're *such* a quitter."

"I am not!" he agitatedly replied as he sat upright.

"You don't act like it." I crossed my arms and shrugged.

He shook his head in disbelief as a smile crept onto his lips. "You're so annoying."

"I take after my older brother." I rolled my eyes. "Why don't you have a break from the time machine? Research something else instead. You need the mental break."

"Like what?"

I sat in silence for a while, thinking about it. *What* should he busy himself with?

"Oh, I know!" I finally piped up. "Me! Study how your invention has affected me. How my foreshadows work; why on earth do I share the same DNA as a flower; why do the foreshadows differ a little; stuff like that."

He sat quietly for a while, thinking it over. "Okay, could work . . . but I'm gonna need details on *everything* you see."

"Consider it done."

"I'm also going to need to track how often you get them, and how differently your brain behaves when you're not here." I could see the familiar enthusiasm finding its way back to his face. "It's going to take weeks of detailed monitoring, but I'm an expert at *that*. This is the next big thing: *Foreshadow Study*."

"Speaking of which," I remembered this morning's foreshadow at the park, "I had one this morning; it was pretty weird."

"What was so weird about it?" He grabbed a notepad and prepared himself.

"That my best friend stole my movie role," Elora said with a frown as she came up the stairs leading to the lab.

"For the millionth time, I did *not* steal your role," I insisted with an eye roll.

"Steal what role?" Mike asked.

I (including interruptions from Elora) told him what I saw this morning during our trip to the city park.

"I see . . ." He stroked his chin in thought. He continued scribbling on his notepad, his eyebrows creased in concentration.

I sat in silence, contemplating the recent events. It was all so crazy. When Mom said high school would be a major turning point in my life, I had no idea it would be *this* wild.

The accident. My bruise. The foreshadows. Elora's near-death. Sarah's birthday. Candy's *actual* death.

I sat glumly and thought about the future. What if it never gets better? What if they drive me insane? What if I can never have a normal life? Then again, when was my life *ever* normal?

I learned to appreciate people a bit more. I learned not to judge people for what they like. I learned that the people closest to you will stand by you no matter what.

And maybe that made my foreshadows worthwhile.

"Why so blue?" Elora asked, a genuine smile on her face; the kind that was reassuring.

"I don't know," I sighed. "The foreshadows, I—"

"It'll be fine." Mike looked up from his work. "You've got us by your side, right?"

"And there's no doubt more insane foreshadows will come your way," Elora added. "But we'll deal with it, *as long as you tell us.*"

I laughed and hugged her, then looked at Mike and felt okay. Maybe these foreshadows weren't as bad as I thought.

I definitely was going to need a ton of support, but it looked like I already had it.

"Now, back to your foreshadow," Mike announced. "Do you think there's potential you'd steal Elora's role or not? Honesty is crucial, so think about it. We can't know for sure, but I might form a hypothesis based on your answer."

For some reason, I hesitated before answering. Uncertainty began flooding me. *Would I* not *take the role? Would I reject it if it was ever offered to me? Would I remain loyal even if I was offered money and fame?*

Of course! She's my best friend and sister, and this is *her* ambition. She's making *her* dream come true, and I'll be by her side, watching her become what she's always wanted. I wouldn't ever do anything to ruin it for her, and definitely not *steal* the role from her . . .

Right?

AFTERWORD

Yay! You finished *Foreshadow*! If you got this far then honestly, I thank you so much for choosing to hide between pages of my imagination and giving me the honor of having you as a reader. I hope it has been fun for you and that all those hours you spent reading instead of studying were worth it. (Don't lie; we all did it at some point. It's bad though, stop it.)

If you just skipped to this page, then be prepared to have the funnest (it's not a word is it) time reading these previous pages, and thank you for choosing to read my book in the first place. If you're reading this as you stand in a bookstore, then thank you for picking out this one out of all the others. (It won't disappoint you though; I promise. There's no such thing as waste in buying a book, right?)

I tried as much as I could to make this novel as relatable as I could. Don't tell me that *not one girl* isn't a Regina George wannabe in your school. (Unless you're a guy. Then I don't know why you're reading this book, but thank you. You do you, bro. Not judging.) Sure, you might not relate, but others probably will. (Hopefully.)

In addition, (yes there's more) every event I had

put in this novel you posses (the *own* kind of posses not the *demon* kind) is relevant in some way. Just find out while you read; it's not that hard. Okay, at some point maybe a little, but I promise this story is more than just a cliché, high school, girl-drama novel. I promise you that. There's so much more between the lines that I wanted to deliver to my readers.

Let me tell you a little about my journey as a teen (sorta) author with this book. Not to educate you and test you about it later on (though if I become a legend that might be necessary. Just kidding; the legendary-est thing I ever did was spend four days in the middle of the forest surrounded by bugs and not die. I'm a wreck in the wilderness.)

I've loved writing since fourth grade. My awesome teachers and amazing mom only made it grow even more; and now I kind of "fangirl" when I talk about writing. It's just an amazing thing; how characters, settings, conflicts … all of it just flows out of your mind and onto a blank slate, waiting to be painted with the colors of a fictional world.

I started working on *Foreshadow* around the end of June 2017 and was gonna pee my pants from excitement. It took *so long*, but it's here! It's been an amazing journey and I'm eternally grateful to everybody involved. From my family and friends' support, to those days spent proofreading and editing, to reading endless articles about first-time authors.

Now, I'm a published author. *At fourteen*. It feels crazy and surreal all at once. I believed the saying "dreams come true", but never *felt* it. Until now. It feels amazing knowing that I've made my dream come true. *It feels great just writing it down.*

It wasn't all smooth-sailing, though. I've met far too much bumps in my road. So many, *so many* people who told me it was a wrong ambition to pursue. So many who told me it isn't a "real job". So many times I felt so unconfident and almost just bailed on *Foreshadow* and walked away. *So many times I felt weak that I almost gave up on my own dream.*

I had to keep reminding myself that I worked too hard to give up. I climbed up too far to go back down. I dreamt too long to back up now. I still had my fears and uncertainties buried inside me; waiting to lash out at any moment. But my parents believed in me, my family believed in me, my friends believed in me, and most importantly, I believed in myself, despite the doubt that still made an appearance every now and then.

Look at me now. I published my first book, despite what everybody had to say about it, whether it was good or bad. My book is in paperback in your hands. It wouldn't have happened if I didn't keep pushing and kept telling myself: *I got this.*

Let that be your living example. Let that be your guide. You're *never* too young to go after your ambition, your passion, your *dream*. Don't let anybody tell you it's too early. Believe in what you can do and do it; maybe you'll be a pioneer in your field. Always remember; you can do it if you believe enough, whether you are fourteen like me, younger or older. It's *never, ever* too early to start doing what you love.

That's how *Foreshadow* came into existence; by persistence, confidence, support, hard work, and most importantly, the blessing from Allah.

Now go out there and chase your dreams; they might not even be as fast-runners as you thought!

If you have anything on your mind you want to tell me, please do. Personally, I get annoyed when I can't find the author's contact, so I saved you the trouble and listed my email, blog and social networking accounts for you …

Instagram - @lalthekair

Twitter - @LAlthekair

Email – leena.thekair@gmail.com

Blog – lalthekair.com

So that's it for now. There are no plans at the moment to make a sequel, but who knows? Meghan might be back for another adventure sooner than you think. Just keep reading, continue being imaginative, and I'll be seeing you (well, you'll be reading) soon.

Stay happy, loves, and keep that smile on your face.

يارب لك الحمد كما ينبغي لجلال وجهك وعظيم سلطانك

يارب لك الحمد، حمدا كثيرا طيبا مطيبا مباركا فيه، ملء السماوات وملء الأرض وملء ما شئت ربي من شيء بعد
...

يارب لك الحمد على نعمك التي انعمت بها علي

الحمد لله الذي رزقني مواهبي

الحمد لله الذي رزقني والدي واعانهم على تربيتي وتنمية موهبتي انا واخوتي

الحمد لله الذي وهبني عائلة تحب الدين والعلم

الحمد لله الذي رزقني رفقاء يدعمونني ويحثوني على فعل كل ما بوسعي

الحمد لله الذي سخر لي مدرستي ومعلماتي اللاتي كان لهن الدور الكبير لبناء جيل يرفع شان الامة الاسلامية

بفضل الله ومنه، تم نشر كتابي الأول.

SPECIAL THANKS

Nu-uh, this isn't your traditional acknowledgements page. This *is* my first book (and I'm a sappy 14-year-old), so don't be too surprised there were a lot of people in on this – and a lot of people I have to thank. A lot of people who cared about this book as much as I did. A lot of people who kept me going, who pushed me along and frankly, I owe them so much. (Warning: cheese. Lots of cheese.)

***

First off, allow me to thank the two most important people in my life; my amazing mom and dad.

Mom kept pushing me from day one. She encouraged me to write ever since I was nine – she was the reason I even realized writing was going to be "my thing". Whenever I had writer's block, she'd help me out. Whenever I fell behind she'd put me back on track. She loved me with all of her heart, and is just as happy as I am that this book is finally out there, for everybody to see. She's really my first best friend and my number one. I love you beyond what words can say; thank you, Abeer.

Dad? He's my partner. I'd write and he'd proofread. He'd help me when I got stuck, advise me when I went wrong, and basically *rocked* the job of being a dad (as well as a manager!) I can't even put into words how much he's awesome, and my eternal gratefulness for him. His dad jokes crack me up; never failing to make me laugh on my worst days. No matter how tired he was, he'd listen to me freaking out and/or fangirling late when he'd come home from work. I love you beyond what words can say; thank you, Nasser.

So, mom, dad. Thank you. I truly feel and appreciate all the sacrifices you've went through for us. All those boring hours spent at work to help me reach my best potential. If I would go on, the pages would be *endless. Everything* you've ever done to me is precious. This book is all thanks to you immediately after Allah. You are the reason I made my dream come true at last. Seeing you smile – seeing you *happy* gives me life. I'd spend all my life to repay you for all you've given me and it still won't be enough.

I'd like to thank my sister. Sure, she's a nuisance and a pain at times, but who's little sister isn't? It's actually funny how I still love her anyways. I'd rant to her about how one character isn't fitting, or ideas I've been considering. She suggested so many improvements and ideas that are priceless. We'd spend night up in bed laughing over something stupid, or baking breakfast in the late afternoons together. She's awesome, lunatic, funny, weird, supportive, and overall a wonderful sister. So Jana, thank you. Okay, my baby sister as well, but she's a year and a half. Thank you anyways, Talah.

I want to thank my entire family. Grandparents, aunts, uncles, cousins, *every single one of you guys.*

Saud and Badiah; my awesome grandparents, who loved me the moment I was a speck in my mom's womb. Zuhoor and Taghreed; my aunts who've been more than my best friends and still are my girl squad. Muhammad, Adbullah, AbdulAziz, and Omar; my uncles, who are the perfect substitute for awesome older brothers who always have my back. Shadi and Joanna; my cousins, who have been the definition of best friends and gave me a wonderful childhood (*which is still ongoing, really*) and priceless memories and moments.

I want to thank my awesome teachers; Mrs. Alima Shakur, Mrs. Lule Bille and Mrs. Nejat Dawood. Never in my life can I forget them. They assigned me writings to challenge me, pointed out my weaknesses and helped me improve them. My passion for writing was born through their and mom's motivation. They were a key factor in helping me become the writer I am today, and I consider myself very honored that they've taught me, and I love them so much.

I want to thank a certain teacher, who hadn't only taught me an invaluable subject; but also, many invaluable life lessons. All the advice, support and laughs you gave me are one of the dearest things I hold close to my heart. You truly are an amazing person, and I love you with all of my heart, Shuoshou.

I want to thank my biggest moral supporter; my best friend. Her excitement and enthusiasm for my book was just as much as mine, and undoubtedly one of the chief reasons this book is between your hands right now. She's been there for me in far more ways than I could mention and honestly means so much to me, and has been the perfect best friend anybody could ask for. I love and owe you so much, Mervat.

I want to thank the awesome-est best friends on the face of the planet. An amazing group of *sisters* that I had the best times of my life with, and frankly, one of the people closest to my heart, and I know I can trust them whenever. For everything; thank you, Ranya, Sadeen, Ghaidaa, and Haya.

Please, let's not forget an awesome group of humans that go by the names of Dana H, Dana A, Fatimah, Hanen, Joody, Ghalia and Rand, not to mention *all* of my **unofficially adoptive family**; you guys rock. I also want to thank Mrs. Nimo, Mrs. Ruqaya and Mrs. Panse. I owe you a whole lot of gratitude and thank-yous for *everything*.

I want to thank Mr. Yasser Bahjatt for helping me through this process and spending all those days reading for me. All those times he's endured my over-enthusiasm and put up with my excitement … Thank you.

I want to thank my book artist for being super friendly and pitching awesome ideas to create the perfect cover. I was always indecisive and nervous, but she assured me it would all be okay. We've grown as friends and, in all seriousness, an amazing human. Thank you, Tala.

I want to thank everybody who ever supported me in any way. Who made me feel better about myself when I felt the worst and kept me going (fam, I'm looking at you). To anyone and everyone who is amazing and is one of the reasons I smile. I'm sorry if I forgot you on these pages, but I promise my heart never will (let's overlook how cheesy that was).

I want to thank once more everybody on the past few pages. *I love you all so much*, and this book is the result of the positive impact you had on me. You mean the world to me, and I am eternally grateful. I hope you remember that the change you caused in me is great, and never forget that this book is partially because of *you*.

Now, I want to thank *you*. Yes *you*. You, who is holding this book in his or her hands. Who has shared their imagination with me and went on an adventure with Meghan. Who was sitting in a corner, my book enveloped between their arms; as the whole world and its noise dissolved into nothingness and they were so caught up in the tale (at least I'm hoping that's what happened). Thank you for choosing to buy my book out of all the better options you had on the shelf. Don't be hesitant at all to reach out to me at any time.

I hope you have enjoyed my tale; and keep a lookout for more stories by yours truly.

Because after all, I was born to write.

xoxo,
leena

Printed in Great Britain
by Amazon